A Caribbean Mystery

HARPER

HARPER

An imprint of HarperCollins*Publishers*
1 London Bridge Street
London SE1 9GF
www.harpercollins.co.uk

This paperback edition 2016

First published in Great Britain by
Collins, The Crime Club 1964

A catalogue record for this book is available from the British Library

ISBN 978-0-00-819660-8

Set in Sabon LT Std by Palimpsest Book Production Limited,
Falkirk, Stirlingshire
Printed and bound in Great Britain

MIX
Paper from
responsible sources

FSC
www.fsc.org   **FSC™ C007454**

To my old friend
John Cruikshank Rose
with happy memories of my
visit to the West Indies

CONTENTS

CHAPTER 1

Major Palgrave Tells a Story

'Take all this business about Kenya,' said Major Palgrave. 'Lots of chaps gabbing away who know nothing about the place! Now *I* spent fourteen years of my life there. Some of the best years of my life, too—'

Old Miss Marple inclined her head.

It was a gentle gesture of courtesy. Whilst Major Palgrave proceeded with the somewhat uninteresting recollections of a lifetime, Miss Marple peacefully pursued her own thoughts. It was a routine with which she was well acquainted. The locale varied. In the past, it had been predominantly India. Majors, Colonels, Lieutenant-Generals—and a familiar series of words: *Simla. Bearers. Tigers. Chota Hazri—Tiffin. Khitmagars*, and so on. With Major Palgrave the terms were slightly different. *Safari. Kikuyu. Elephants. Swahili*. But the pattern was essentially the same. An elderly man who needed a listener so that he could, in memory, relive days in which he had been happy. Days when his back had been straight, his eyesight keen, his hearing acute.

1

Some of these talkers had been handsome soldierly old boys, some again had been regrettably unattractive; and Major Palgrave, purple of face, with a glass eye, and the general appearance of a stuffed frog, belonged in the latter category.

Miss Marple had bestowed on all of them the same gentle charity. She had sat attentively, inclining her head from time to time in gentle agreement, thinking her own thoughts and enjoying what there was to enjoy: in this case the deep blue of a Caribbean Sea.

So kind of dear Raymond—she was thinking gratefully, so really and truly kind . . . Why he should take so much trouble about his old aunt, she really did not know. Conscience, perhaps; family feeling? Or possibly he was truly fond of her . . .

She thought, on the whole, that he *was* fond of her—he always had been—in a slightly exasperated and contemptuous way! Always trying to bring her up to date. Sending her books to read. Modern novels. So difficult—all about such unpleasant people, doing such very odd things and not, apparently, even enjoying them. 'Sex' as a word had not been mentioned in Miss Marple's young days; but there had been plenty of it—not talked about so much—but enjoyed far more than nowadays, or so it seemed to her. Though usually labelled Sin, she couldn't help feeling that that was preferable to what it seemed to be nowadays—a kind of Duty.

Her glance strayed for a moment to the book on her lap lying open at page twenty-three which was as far as she had got (and indeed as far as she felt like getting!).

'"Do you mean that you've had no sexual experience at ALL?" demanded the young man incredulously. "At *nineteen*? But you *must*. It's vital."

'The girl hung her head unhappily, her straight greasy hair fell forward over her face.

'"I know," she muttered, "I know."

'He looked at her, stained old jersey, the bare feet, the dirty toe nails, the smell of rancid fat . . . He wondered why he found her so maddeningly attractive.'

Miss Marple wondered too! And really! To have sex experience urged on you exactly as though it was an iron tonic! Poor young things . . .

'My dear Aunt Jane, why must you bury your head in the sand like a very delightful ostrich? All bound up in this idyllic rural life of yours. REAL LIFE—that's what matters.'

Thus Raymond—and his Aunt Jane had looked properly abashed—and said 'Yes,' she was afraid she *was* rather old-fashioned.

Though really rural life was far from idyllic. People like Raymond were so ignorant. In the course of her duties in a country parish, Jane Marple had acquired quite a comprehensive knowledge of the facts of rural life. She had no urge to *talk* about them, far less to *write* about them—but she knew them. Plenty of sex, natural and unnatural. Rape, incest, perversion of all kinds. (Some kinds, indeed, that even the clever young men from Oxford who wrote books didn't seem to have heard about.)

Miss Marple came back to the Caribbean and took up the thread of what Major Palgrave was saying . . .

'A very unusual experience,' she said encouragingly. '*Most* interesting.'

'I could tell you a lot more. Some of the things, of course, not fit for a lady's ears—'

With the ease of long practice, Miss Marple dropped her eyelids in a fluttery fashion, and Major Palgrave continued his bowdlerized version of tribal customs whilst Miss Marple resumed her thoughts of her affectionate nephew.

Raymond West was a very successful novelist and made a large income, and he conscientiously and kindly did all he could to alleviate the life of his elderly aunt. The preceding winter she had had a bad go of pneumonia, and medical opinion had advised sunshine. In lordly fashion Raymond had suggested a trip to the West Indies. Miss Marple had demurred—at the expense, the distance, the difficulties of travel, and at abandoning her house in St Mary Mead. Raymond had dealt with everything. A friend who was writing a book wanted a quiet place in the country. 'He'll look after the house all right. He's very house proud. He's a queer. I mean—'

He had paused, slightly embarrassed—but surely even dear old Aunt Jane must have heard of queers.

He went on to deal with the next points. Travel was nothing nowadays. She would go by air—another friend, Diana Horrocks, was going out to Trinidad and would see Aunt Jane was all right as far as there, and at St Honoré she would stay at the Golden Palm Hotel which was run by the Sandersons. Nicest couple in the world. They'd see she was all right. He'd write to them straight away.

As it happened the Sandersons had returned to England. But their successors, the Kendals, had been very nice and friendly and had assured Raymond that he need have no qualms about his aunt. There was a very good doctor on the island in case of emergency and they themselves would keep an eye on her and see to her comfort.

They had been as good as their word, too. Molly Kendal was an ingenuous blonde of twenty odd, always apparently in good spirits. She had greeted the old lady warmly and did everything to make her comfortable. Tim Kendal, her husband, lean, dark and in his thirties, had also been kindness itself.

So there she was, thought Miss Marple, far from the rigours of the English climate, with a nice bungalow of her own, with friendly smiling West Indian girls to wait on her, Tim Kendal to meet her in the dining-room and crack a joke as he advised her about the day's menu, and an easy path from her bungalow to the sea front and the bathing beach where she could sit in a comfortable basket chair and watch the bathing. There were even a few elderly guests for company. Old Mr Rafiel, Dr Graham, Canon Prescott and his sister, and her present cavalier Major Palgrave.

What more could an elderly lady want?

It is deeply to be regretted, and Miss Marple felt guilty even admitting it to herself, but she was not as satisfied as she ought to be.

Lovely and warm, yes—and *so* good for her rheumatism—and beautiful scenery, though perhaps—a trifle monotonous? So *many* palm trees. Everything the same

5

every day—never anything *happening*. Not like St Mary Mead where something was always happening. Her nephew had once compared life in St Mary Mead to scum on a pond, and she had indignantly pointed out that smeared on a slide under the microscope there would be plenty of life to be observed. Yes, indeed, in St Mary Mead, there was always something going on. Incident after incident flashed through Miss Marple's mind, the mistake in old Mrs Linnett's cough mixture—that very odd behaviour of young Polegate—the time when Georgy Wood's mother had come down to see him—(but *was* she his mother—?) the real cause of the quarrel between Joe Arden and his wife. So many interesting human problems—giving rise to endless pleasurable hours of speculation. If only there were something here that she could—well—get her teeth into.

With a start she realized that Major Palgrave had abandoned Kenya for the North West Frontier and was relating his experiences as a subaltern. Unfortunately he was asking her with great earnestness: 'Now don't you agree?'

Long practice had made Miss Marple quite an adept at dealing with that one.

'I don't really feel that I've got sufficient experience to judge. I'm afraid I've led rather a sheltered life.'

'And so you should, dear lady, so you should,' cried Major Palgrave gallantly.

'You've had such a very varied life,' went on Miss Marple, determined to make amends for her former pleasurable inattention.

'Not bad,' said Major Palgrave, complacently. 'Not bad

at all.' He looked round him appreciatively. 'Lovely place, this.'

'Yes, indeed,' said Miss Marple and was then unable to stop herself going on: 'Does anything ever happen here, I wonder?'

Major Palgrave stared.

'Oh rather. Plenty of scandals—eh what? Why, I could tell you—'

But it wasn't really scandals Miss Marple wanted. Nothing to get your teeth into in scandals nowadays. Just men and women changing partners, and calling attention to it, instead of trying decently to hush it up and be properly ashamed of themselves.

'There was even a murder here a couple of years ago. Man called Harry Western. Made a big splash in the papers. Dare say you remember it.'

Miss Marple nodded without enthusiasm. It had not been her kind of murder. It had made a big splash mainly because everyone concerned had been very rich. It had seemed likely enough that Harry Western had shot the Count de Ferrari, his wife's lover, and equally likely that his well-arranged alibi had been bought and paid for. Everyone seemed to have been drunk, and there was a fine scattering of dope addicts. Not really interesting people, thought Miss Marple—although no doubt very spectacular and attractive to *look* at. But definitely not *her* cup of tea.

'And if you ask me, that wasn't the only murder about that time.' He nodded and winked. 'I had my suspicions—oh!—well—'

7

Agatha Christie

Miss Marple dropped her ball of wool, and the Major stooped and picked it up for her.

'Talking of murder,' he went on. 'I once came across a very curious case—not exactly personally.'

Miss Marple smiled encouragingly.

'Lot of chaps talking at the club one day, you know, and a chap began telling a story. Medical man he was. One of his cases. Young fellow came and knocked him up in the middle of the night. His wife had hanged herself. They hadn't got a telephone, so after the chap had cut her down and done what he could, he'd got out his car and hared off looking for a doctor. Well, she wasn't dead but pretty far gone. Anyway, she pulled through. Young fellow seemed devoted to her. Cried like a child. He'd noticed that she'd been odd for some time, fits of depression and all that. Well, that was that. Everything seemed all right. But actually, about a month later, the wife took an overdose of sleeping stuff and passed out. Sad case.'

Major Palgrave paused, and nodded his head several times. Since there was obviously more to come Miss Marple waited.

'And that's that, you might say. Nothing there. Neurotic woman, nothing out of the usual. But about a year later, this medical chap was swapping yarns with a fellow medico, and the other chap told him about a woman who'd tried to drown herself, husband got her out, got a doctor, they pulled her round—and then a few weeks later she gassed herself.

'Well, a bit of a coincidence—eh? Same sort of story. My chap said—"I had a case rather like that. Name of Jones

8

(or whatever the name was)—What was your man's name?"
"Can't remember. Robinson I think. Certainly not Jones."

'Well, the chaps looked at each other and said it was pretty odd. And then my chap pulled out a snapshot. He showed it to the second chap. "That's the fellow," he said— "I'd gone along the next day to check up on the particulars, and I noticed a magnificent species of hibiscus just by the front door, a variety I'd never seen before in this country. My camera was in the car and I took a photo. Just as I snapped the shutter the husband came out of the front door so I got him as well. Don't think he realized it. I asked him about the hibiscus but he couldn't tell me its name." Second medico looked at the snap. He said: "It's a bit out of focus—But I could swear—at any rate I'm almost sure—*it's the same man*."

'Don't know if they followed it up. But if so they didn't get anywhere. Expect Mr Jones or Robinson covered his tracks too well. But queer story, isn't it? Wouldn't think things like that could happen.'

'Oh, yes, I would,' said Miss Marple placidly. 'Practically every day.'

'Oh, come, come. That's a bit fantastic.'

'If a man gets a formula that works—he won't stop. He'll go on.'

'Brides in the bath—eh?'

'That kind of thing, yes.'

'Doctor let me have that snap just as a curiosity—'

Major Palgrave began fumbling through an overstuffed wallet murmuring to himself: 'Lots of things in here—don't know why I keep all these things . . .'

Miss Marple thought she did know. They were part of the Major's stock-in-trade. They illustrated his repertoire of stories. The story he had just told, or so she suspected, had not been originally like that—it had been worked up a good deal in repeated telling.

The Major was still shuffling and muttering—'Forgotten all about *that* business. Good-looking woman *she* was, you'd never suspect—now *where*—Ah—that takes my mind back—what tusks! I must show you—'

He stopped—sorted out a small photographic print and peered down at it.

'Like to see the picture of a murderer?'

He was about to pass it to her when his movement was suddenly arrested. Looking more like a stuffed frog than ever, Major Palgrave appeared to be staring fixedly over her right shoulder—from whence came the sound of approaching footsteps and voices.

'Well, I'm damned—I mean—' He stuffed everything back into his wallet and crammed it into his pocket.

His face went an even deeper shade of purplish red—He exclaimed in a loud, artificial voice:

'As I was saying—I'd like to have shown you those elephant tusks—Biggest elephant I've ever shot—Ah, hallo!' His voice took on a somewhat spurious hearty note.

'Look who's here! The great quartette—Flora and Fauna—What luck have you had today—Eh?'

The approaching footsteps resolved themselves into four of the hotel guests whom Miss Marple already knew by sight. They consisted of two married couples and though Miss Marple was not as yet acquainted with their surnames, she knew that the big man with the upstanding bush of thick grey hair was addressed as 'Greg', that the golden blonde woman, his wife, was known as Lucky— and that the other married couple, the dark lean man and the handsome but rather weather-beaten woman, were Edward and Evelyn. They were botanists, she understood, and also interested in birds.

'No luck at all,' said Greg—'At least no luck in getting what we were after.'

'Don't know if you know Miss Marple? Colonel and Mrs Hillingdon and Greg and Lucky Dyson.'

They greeted her pleasantly and Lucky said loudly that she'd die if she didn't have a drink at once or sooner.

Greg hailed Tim Kendal who was sitting a little way away with his wife poring over account books.

'Hi, Tim. Get us some drinks.' He addressed the others. 'Planters Punch?'

They agreed.

'Same for you, Miss Marple?'

Miss Marple said Thank you, but she would prefer fresh lime.

'Fresh lime it is,' said Tim Kendal, 'and five Planters Punches.'

'Join us, Tim?'

'Wish I could. But I've got to fix up these accounts. Can't leave Molly to cope with everything. Steel band tonight, by the way.'

'Good,' cried Lucky. 'Damn it,' she winced, 'I'm all over thorns. Ouch! Edward deliberately rammed me into a thorn bush!'

'Lovely pink flowers,' said Hillingdon.

'And lovely long thorns. Sadistic brute, aren't you, Edward?'

'Not like me,' said Greg, grinning. 'Full of the milk of human kindness.'

Evelyn Hillingdon sat down by Miss Marple and started talking to her in an easy pleasant way.

Miss Marple put her knitting down on her lap. Slowly and with some difficulty, owing to rheumatism in the neck, she turned her head over her right shoulder to look behind her. At some little distance there was the large bungalow occupied by the rich Mr Rafiel. But it showed no sign of life.

She replied suitably to Evelyn's remarks (really, how kind people were to her!) but her eyes scanned thoughtfully the faces of the two men.

Edward Hillingdon looked a nice man. Quiet but with a lot of charm . . . And Greg—big, boisterous, happy-looking. He and Lucky were Canadian or American, she thought.

She looked at Major Palgrave, still acting a *bonhomie* a little larger than life.

Interesting . . .

CHAPTER 2

Miss Marple Makes Comparisons

It was very gay that evening at the Golden Palm Hotel.

Seated at her little corner table, Miss Marple looked round her in an interested fashion. The dining-room was a large room open on three sides to the soft warm scented air of the West Indies. There were small table lamps, all softly coloured. Most of the women were in evening dress: light cotton prints out of which bronzed shoulders and arms emerged. Miss Marple herself had been urged by her nephew's wife, Joan, in the sweetest way possible, to accept 'a small cheque'.

'Because, Aunt Jane, it will be rather hot out there, and I don't expect you have any very thin clothes.'

Jane Marple had thanked her and had accepted the cheque. She came of the age when it was natural for the old to support and finance the young, but also for the middle-aged to look after the old. She could not, however, force herself to buy anything very *thin*! At her age she seldom felt more than pleasantly warm even in the hottest weather, and the temperature of St Honoré was not really what is referred to as 'tropical heat'. This evening she was attired in the best traditions of the provincial gentlewoman of England—grey lace.

Not that she was the only elderly person present. There were representatives of all ages in the room. There were elderly tycoons with young third or fourth wives. There were middle-aged couples from the North of England. There was a gay family from Caracas complete with children. The various countries of South America were well represented, all chattering loudly in Spanish or Portuguese. There was a solid English background of two clergymen, one doctor and one retired judge. There was even a family of Chinese. The dining-room service was mainly done by women, tall black girls of proud carriage, dressed in crisp white; but there was an experienced Italian head waiter in charge, and a French wine waiter, and there was the attentive eye of Tim Kendal watching over everything, pausing here and there to have a social word with people at their tables. His wife seconded him ably. She was a good-looking girl. Her hair was a natural golden blonde and she had a wide generous mouth that laughed easily. It was very seldom that Molly Kendal was out of temper. Her staff worked for her enthusiastically, and she adapted her manner carefully to suit her different guests. With the elderly men she laughed and flirted; she congratulated the younger women on their clothes.

'Oh, what a smashing dress you've got on tonight, Mrs Dyson. I'm so jealous I could tear it off your back.' But she looked very well in her own dress, or so Miss Marple thought: a white sheath, with a pale green embroidered silk shawl thrown over her shoulders. Lucky was fingering the shawl. 'Lovely colour! I'd like one like it.' 'You can get them at the shop here,' Molly told her and passed on. She did not pause by Miss Marple's table. Elderly ladies she usually left to her husband. 'The old dears like a man much better,' she used to say.

Tim Kendal came and bent over Miss Marple.

'Nothing special you want, is there?' he asked. 'Because you've only got to tell me—and I could get it specially cooked for you. Hotel food, and semi-tropical at that, isn't quite what you're used to at home, I expect?'

Miss Marple smiled and said that that was one of the pleasures of coming abroad.

'That's all right, then. But if there *is* anything—'

'Such as?'

'Well—' Tim Kendal looked a little doubtful—'Bread and butter pudding?' he hazarded.

Miss Marple smiled and said that she thought she could do without bread and butter pudding very nicely for the present.

She picked up her spoon and began to eat her passion fruit sundae with cheerful appreciation.

Then the steel band began to play. The steel bands were one of the main attractions of the islands. Truth to tell, Miss Marple could have done very well without them. She considered that they made a hideous noise, unnecessarily loud. The pleasure that everyone else took in them was undeniable, however, and Miss Marple, in the true spirit of her youth, decided that as they had to be, she must manage somehow to learn to like them. She could hardly request Tim Kendal to conjure up from somewhere the muted strains of the 'Blue Danube'. (So graceful—waltzing.) Most peculiar, the way people danced nowadays. Flinging themselves about, seeming quite *contorted*. Oh well, young people must enjoy—Her thoughts were arrested. Because, now she came to think of it, very few of these people *were* young. Dancing, lights, the music of a band (even a steel band), all that surely was for *youth*. But where was youth? Studying, she supposed, at universities, or doing a job—with a fortnight's holiday a year. A place like this was too far away and too expensive. This gay and carefree life was all for the thirties and the forties—and the old men who were trying to live up (or down) to their young wives. It seemed, somehow, a *pity*.

Miss Marple sighed for youth. There was Mrs Kendal, of course. She wasn't more than twenty-two or three, probably, and she seemed to be enjoying herself—but even so, it was a *job* she was doing.

At a table nearby Canon Prescott and his sister were sitting. They motioned to Miss Marple to join them for coffee and she did so. Miss Prescott was a thin severe-looking woman, the Canon was a round, rubicund man, breathing geniality.

Coffee was brought, and chairs were pushed a little way away from the tables. Miss Prescott opened a work bag and took out some frankly hideous table mats that she was hemming. She told Miss Marple all about the day's events. They had visited a new Girls' School in the morning. After an afternoon's rest, they had walked through a cane plantation to have tea at a *pension* where some friends of theirs were staying.

Since the Prescotts had been at the Golden Palm longer than Miss Marple, they were able to enlighten her as to some of her fellow guests.

That very old man, Mr Rafiel. He came every year. Fantastically rich! Owned an enormous chain of super-markets in the North of England. The young woman with him was his secretary, Esther Walters—a widow. (Quite all *right*, of course. Nothing improper. After all, he was nearly eighty!)

Miss Marple accepted the propriety of the relationship with an understanding nod and the Canon remarked:

'A very nice young woman; her mother, I understand, is a widow and lives in Chichester.'

'Mr Rafiel has a valet with him, too. Or rather a kind of Nurse Attendant—he's a qualified masseur, I believe. Jackson, his name is. Poor Mr Rafiel is practically paralysed. So sad—with all that money, too.'

'A generous and cheerful giver,' said Canon Prescott approvingly.

People were regrouping themselves round about, some going farther from the steel band, others crowding up to it. Major Palgrave had joined the Hillingdon-Dyson quartette.

'Now those people—' said Miss Prescott, lowering her voice quite unnecessarily since the steel band easily drowned it.

'Yes, I was going to ask you about them.'

'They were here last year. They spend three months

17

every year in the West Indies, going round the different islands. The tall thin man is Colonel Hillingdon and the dark woman is his wife—they are botanists. The other two, Mr and Mrs Gregory Dyson—they're American. He writes on butterflies, I believe. And all of them are interested in birds.'

'So nice for people to have open-air hobbies,' said Canon Prescott genially.

'I don't think they'd like to hear you call it hobbies, Jeremy,' said his sister. 'They have articles printed in the *National Geographic* and in the *Royal Horticultural Journal*. They take themselves very seriously.'

A loud outburst of laughter came from the table they had been observing. It was loud enough to overcome the steel band. Gregory Dyson was leaning back in his chair and thumping the table, his wife was protesting, and Major Palgrave emptied his glass and seemed to be applauding.

They hardly qualified for the moment as people who took themselves seriously.

'Major Palgrave should not drink so much,' said Miss Prescott acidly. 'He has blood pressure.'

A fresh supply of Planters Punches was brought to the table.

'It's so nice to get people sorted out,' said Miss Marple. 'When I met them this afternoon I wasn't sure which was married to which.'

There was a slight pause. Miss Prescott coughed a small dry cough, and said—'Well, as to that—'

'Joan,' said the Canon in an admonitory voice. 'Perhaps it would be wise to say no more.'

'Really, Jeremy, I wasn't going to say *anything*. Only that last year, for some reason or other—I really don't know *why*—we got the idea that Mrs Dyson was Mrs Hillingdon until someone told us she wasn't.'

'It's odd how one gets impressions, isn't it?' said Miss Marple innocently. Her eyes met Miss Prescott's for a moment. A flash of womanly understanding passed between them.

A more sensitive man than Canon Prescott might have felt that he was *de trop*.

Another signal passed between the women. It said as clearly as if the words had been spoken: '*Some other time . . .*'

'Mr Dyson calls his wife "Lucky". Is that her real name or a nickname?' asked Miss Marple.

'It can hardly be her real name, I should think.'

'I happened to ask him,' said the Canon. 'He said he called her Lucky because she was his good-luck piece. If he lost her, he said, he'd lose his luck. Very nicely put, I thought.'

'He's very fond of joking,' said Miss Prescott.

The Canon looked at his sister doubtfully.

The steel band outdid itself with a wild burst of cacophony and a troupe of dancers came racing on to the floor.

Miss Marple and the others turned their chairs to watch. Miss Marple enjoyed the dancing better than the music; she liked the shuffling feet and the rhythmic sway of the bodies. It seemed, she thought, very *real*. It had a kind of power of understatement.

Tonight, for the first time, she began to feel slightly at home in her new environment . . . Up to now, she had missed what she usually found so easy, points of resemblance in the people she met, to various people known to her personally. She had, possibly, been dazzled by the gay clothes and the exotic colouring; but soon, she felt, she would be able to make some interesting comparisons.

Molly Kendal, for instance, was like that nice girl whose name she couldn't remember, but who was a conductress on the Market Basing bus. Helped you in, and never rang the bus on until she was sure you'd sat down safely. Tim Kendal was just a little like the head waiter at the Royal George in Medchester. Self-confident, and yet, at the same time, worried. (He had had an ulcer, she remembered.) As for Major Palgrave, he was undistinguishable from General Leroy, Captain Flemming, Admiral Wicklow and Commander Richardson. She went on to someone more interesting. Greg for instance? Greg was difficult because he was American. A dash of Sir George Trollope, perhaps, always so full of jokes at the Civil Defence meetings—or perhaps Mr Murdoch the butcher. Mr Murdoch had had rather a bad reputation, but some people said it was just gossip, and that Mr Murdoch himself liked to encourage the rumours! 'Lucky' now? Well, that was easy—Marleen at the Three Crowns. Evelyn Hillingdon? She couldn't fit Evelyn in precisely. In appearance she fitted many roles— tall thin weather-beaten Englishwomen were plentiful. Lady Caroline Wolfe, Peter Wolfe's first wife, who had committed suicide? Or there was Leslie James—that quiet woman who seldom showed what she felt and who had sold up her house and left without ever telling anyone she was going. Colonel Hillingdon? No immediate clue there. She'd have to get to know him a little first. One of those quiet men with good manners. You never knew what they were thinking about. Sometimes they surprised you. Major Harper, she remembered, had quietly cut his throat one day. Nobody had ever known why. Miss Marple thought that she did know—but she'd never been quite sure . . .

Her eyes strayed to Mr Rafiel's table. The principal thing known about Mr Rafiel was that he was incredibly rich, he came every year to the West Indies, he was semi-paralysed and looked like a wrinkled old bird of prey. His clothes hung loosely on his shrunken form. He might have been seventy or eighty, or even ninety. His eyes were shrewd and he was frequently rude, but people seldom took offence, partly because he was so rich, and partly because of his overwhelming personality which hypnotized you into feeling that somehow, Mr Rafiel had the right to be rude if he wanted to.

With him sat his secretary, Mrs Walters. She had corn-coloured hair, and a pleasant face. Mr Rafiel was frequently very rude to her, but she never seemed to notice it—She was not so much subservient, as oblivious. She behaved like a well-trained hospital nurse. Possibly, thought Miss Marple, she had been a hospital nurse.

A young man, tall and good-looking, in a white jacket, came to stand by Mr Rafiel's chair. The old man looked up at him, nodded, then motioned him to a chair. The young man sat down as bidden. 'Mr Jackson, I presume,' said Miss Marple to herself—'His valet-attendant.'

She studied Mr Jackson with some attention.

In the bar, Molly Kendal stretched her back, and slipped off her high-heeled shoes. Tim came in from the terrace to join her. They had the bar to themselves for the moment.

'Tired, darling?' he asked.

'Just a bit. I seem to be feeling my feet tonight.'

'Not too much for you, is it? All this? I know it's hard work.' He looked at her anxiously.

She laughed. 'Oh, Tim, don't be ridiculous. I love it here. It's gorgeous. The kind of dream I've always had, come true.'

'Yes, it would be all right—if one was just a guest. But running the show—that's work.'

'Well, you can't have anything for nothing, can you?' said Molly Kendal reasonably.

Tim Kendal frowned.

'You think it's going all right? A success? We're making a go of it?'

'Of course we are.'

'You don't think people are saying, "It's not the same as when the Sandersons were here"?'

'Of course *someone* will be saying that—they always do! But only some old stick-in-the-mud. I'm sure that we're far better at the job than they were. We're more glamorous. You charm the old pussies and manage to look as though you'd like to make love to the desperate forties and fifties, and I ogle the old gentlemen and make them feel sexy dogs—or play the sweet little daughter the sentimental ones would love to have had. Oh, we've got it all taped splendidly.'

Tim's frown vanished.

'As long as *you* think so. I get scared. We've risked everything on making a job of this. I chucked my job—'

'And quite right to do so,' Molly put in quickly. 'It was soul-destroying.'

He laughed and kissed the tip of her nose.

'I tell you we've got it taped,' she repeated. 'Why do you always worry?'

'Made that way, I suppose. I'm always thinking—suppose something should go wrong?'

'What sort of thing—'

'Oh, I don't know. Somebody might get drowned.'

'Not they. It's one of the safest of all the beaches. And we've got that hulking Swede always on guard.'

'I'm a fool,' said Tim Kendal. He hesitated—and then said, 'You—haven't had any more of those dreams, have you?'

'That was shellfish,' said Molly, and laughed.

CHAPTER 3

A Death in the Hotel

Miss Marple had her breakfast brought to her in bed as usual. Tea, a boiled egg, and a slice of paw-paw.

The fruit on the island, thought Miss Marple, was rather disappointing. It seemed always to be paw-paw. If she could have a nice apple now—but apples seemed to be unknown.

Now that she had been here a week, Miss Marple had cured herself of the impulse to ask what the weather was like. The weather was always the same—fine. No interesting variations.

'The many splendoured weather of an English day,' she murmured to herself and wondered if it was a quotation, or whether she had made it up.

There were, of course, hurricanes, or so she understood. But hurricanes were not weather in Miss Marple's sense of the word. They were more in the nature of an Act of God. There was rain, short violent rainfall that lasted five minutes and stopped abruptly. Everything and everyone was wringing wet, but in another five minutes they were dry again.

The black West Indian girl smiled and said Good Morning as she placed the tray on Miss Marple's knees. Such lovely white teeth and so happy and smiling. Nice natures, all these girls, and a pity they were so averse to getting married. It worried Canon Prescott a good deal. Plenty of christenings, he said, trying to console himself, but no weddings.

Miss Marple ate her breakfast and decided how she would spend her day. It didn't really take much deciding. She would get up at her leisure, moving slowly because it was rather hot and her fingers weren't as nimble as they used to be. Then she would rest for ten minutes or so, and she would take her knitting and walk slowly along towards the hotel and decide where she would settle herself. On the terrace overlooking the sea? Or should she go on to the bathing beach to watch the bathers and the children? Usually it was the latter. In the afternoon, after her rest, she might take a drive. It really didn't matter very much.

Today would be a day like any other day, she said to herself.

Only, of course, it wasn't.

Miss Marple carried out her programme as planned and was slowly making her way along the path towards the hotel when she met Molly Kendal. For once that sunny young woman was not smiling. Her air of distress was so unlike her that Miss Marple said immediately:

'My dear, is anything wrong?'

Molly nodded. She hesitated and then said: 'Well, you'll have to know—everyone will have to know. It's Major Palgrave. He's dead.'

'Dead?'

'Yes. He died in the night.'

'Oh, dear, I *am* sorry.'

'Yes, it's horrid having a death here. It makes everyone depressed. Of course—he *was* quite old.'

'He seemed quite well and cheerful yesterday,' said Miss Marple, slightly resenting this calm assumption that everyone of advanced years was liable to die at any minute.

'He seemed quite healthy,' she added.

'He had high blood pressure,' said Molly.

'But surely there are things one takes nowadays—some kind of pill. Science is so wonderful.'

'Oh yes, but perhaps he forgot to take his pills, or took too many of them. Like insulin, you know.'

Miss Marple did not think that diabetes and high blood pressure were at all the same kind of thing. She asked:

'What does the doctor say?'

'Oh, Dr Graham, who's practically retired now, and lives in the hotel, took a look at him, and the local people came officially, of course, to give a death certificate, but it all seems quite straightforward. This kind of thing is quite liable to happen when you have high blood pressure, especially if you overdo the alcohol, and Major Palgrave was really very naughty that way. Last night, for instance.'

'Yes, I noticed,' said Miss Marple.

'He probably forgot to take his pills. It is bad luck for the old boy—but people can't live for ever, can they? But it's terribly worrying—for me and Tim, I mean. People might suggest it was something in the food.'

'But surely the symptoms of food poisoning and of blood pressure are *quite* different?'

'Yes. But people do *say* things so easily. And if people decided the food was bad—and left—or told their friends—'

'I really don't think you need worry,' said Miss Marple kindly. 'As you say, an elderly man like Major Palgrave—he must have been over seventy—is quite liable to die. To most people it will seem quite an ordinary occurrence—sad, but not out of the way at all.'

'If only,' said Molly unhappily, 'it hadn't been so *sudden*.'

Yes, it had been very sudden, Miss Marple thought as she walked slowly on. There he had been last night, laughing and talking in the best of spirits with the Hillingdons and the Dysons.

The Hillingdons and the Dysons . . . Miss Marple walked more slowly still . . . Finally she stopped abruptly. Instead of going to the bathing beach she settled herself in a shady corner of the terrace. She took out her knitting and the needles clicked rapidly as though they were trying to match the speed of her thoughts. *She didn't like it—no, she didn't like it. It came so pat.*

She went over the occurrences of yesterday in her mind. Major Palgrave and his stories . . .

That was all as usual and one didn't need to listen very closely . . . Perhaps, though, it would have been better if she had.

Kenya—he had talked about Kenya and then India—the North West Frontier—and then—for some reason they had got on to murder—And even *then* she hadn't really been listening . . .

Some famous case that had taken place out here—that had been in the newspapers—

It was after that—when he picked up her ball of wool—that he had begun telling her about a snapshot—*A snapshot of a murderer*—that is what he had said.

Miss Marple closed her eyes and tried to remember just exactly how that story had gone.

It had been rather a confused story—told to the Major in his club—or in somebody else's club—told him by a doctor—who had heard it from another doctor—and one doctor had taken a snapshot of someone coming through a front door—someone who was a murderer—

Yes, that was it—the various details were coming back to her now—

And he had offered to show her that snapshot—He had got out his wallet and begun hunting through its contents—talking all the time . . .

And then still talking, he had looked up—had looked—not at her—but at something behind her—behind her right shoulder to be accurate. And he had stopped talking, his face had gone purple—and he had started stuffing back everything into his wallet with slightly shaky hands and had begun talking in a loud unnatural voice about elephant tusks!

A moment or two later the Hillingdons and the Dysons had joined them . . .

It was then that she had turned her head over her right shoulder to look . . . But there had been nothing and nobody to see. To her left, some distance away, in the direction of the hotel, there had been Tim Kendal and his wife; and beyond them a family group of Venezuelans. But Major Palgrave had not been looking in that direction . . .

Miss Marple meditated until lunch time.

After lunch she did not go for a drive.

Instead she sent a message to say that she was not feeling very well and to ask if Dr Graham would be kind enough to come and see her.

CHAPTER 4

Miss Marple Seeks Medical Attention

Dr Graham was a kindly elderly man of about sixty-five. He had practised in the West Indies for many years, but was now semi-retired, and left most of his work to his West Indian partners. He greeted Miss Marple pleasantly and asked her what the trouble was. Fortunately at Miss Marple's age, there was always some ailment that could be discussed with slight exaggerations on the patient's part. Miss Marple hesitated between 'her shoulder' and 'her knee', but finally decided upon the knee. Miss Marple's knee, as she would have put it to herself, was always with her.

Dr Graham was exceedingly kindly but he refrained from putting into words the fact that at her time of life such troubles were only to be expected. He prescribed for her one of the brands of useful little pills that form the basis of a doctor's prescriptions. Since he knew by experience that many elderly people could be lonely when they first came to St Honoré, he remained for a while gently chatting.

'A very nice man,' thought Miss Marple to herself, 'and I really feel rather ashamed of having to tell him lies. But I don't quite see what else I can do.'

Miss Marple had been brought up to have a proper regard for truth and was indeed by nature a very truthful person. But on certain occasions, when she considered it her duty so to do, she could tell lies with a really astonishing verisimilitude.

She cleared her throat, uttered an apologetic little cough, and said, in an old ladyish and slightly twittering manner:

'There is something, Dr Graham, I would like to ask you. I don't really like mentioning it—but I don't quite see what else I am to do—although of course it's *quite* unimportant really. But you see, it's important to *me*. And I hope you will understand and not think what I am asking is tiresome or—or unpardonable in any way.'

To this opening Dr Graham replied kindly: 'Something is worrying you? Do let me help.'

'It's connected with Major Palgrave. *So* sad about his dying. It was quite a shock when I heard it this morning.'

'Yes,' said Dr Graham, 'it was very sudden, I'm afraid. He seemed in such good spirits yesterday.' He spoke kindly, but conventionally. To him, clearly, Major Palgrave's death was nothing out of the way. Miss Marple wondered whether she was really making something out of nothing. Was this suspicious habit of mind growing on her? Perhaps she could no longer trust her own judgment. Not that it was judgment really, only suspicion. Anyway she was in for it now! She must go ahead.

'We were sitting talking together yesterday afternoon,' she said. 'He was telling me about his very varied and interesting life. So many strange parts of the globe.'

'Yes indeed,' said Dr Graham, who had been bored many times by the Major's reminiscences.

'And then he spoke of his family, boyhood rather, and I told him a little about my own nephews and nieces and he listened very sympathetically. And I showed him a snapshot I had with me of one of my nephews. Such a dear boy—at least not exactly a boy now, but always a boy to *me* if you understand.'

'Quite so,' said Dr Graham, wondering how long it would be before the old lady was going to come to the point.

'I had handed it to him and he was examining it when quite suddenly those people—those very nice people—who collect wild flowers and butterflies, Colonel and Mrs Hillingdon I think the name is—'

'Oh yes? The Hillingdons and the Dysons.'

'Yes, that's right. They came suddenly along laughing and talking. They sat down and ordered drinks and we all talked together. Very pleasant it was. But without thinking, Major Palgrave must have put back my snapshot into his wallet and returned it to his pocket. I wasn't paying very much attention at the time but I remembered afterward and I said to myself—"I mustn't forget to ask the Major to give me back my picture of Denzil." I *did* think of it last night while the dancing and the band was going on, but I didn't like to interrupt him just then, because they were having such a merry party together

32

and I thought "I will remember to ask him for it in the morning." Only this morning—' Miss Marple paused—out of breath.

'Yes, yes,' said Dr Graham, 'I quite understand. And you—well, naturally you want the snapshot back. Is that it?'

Miss Marple nodded her head in eager agreement.

'Yes. That's it. You see, it is the only one I have got and I haven't got the negative. And I would hate to lose that snapshot, because poor Denzil died some five or six years ago and he was my favourite nephew. This is the only picture I have to remind me of him. I wondered—I hoped—it is rather tiresome of me to ask—whether you could possibly manage to get hold of it for me? I don't really know who else to ask, you see. I don't know who'll attend to all his belongings and things like that. It is all so difficult. They would think it such a nuisance of me. You see, they don't understand. Nobody could quite understand what this snapshot means to me.'

'Of course, of course,' said Dr Graham. 'I quite understand. A most natural feeling on your part. Actually, I am meeting the local authorities shortly—the funeral is tomorrow—and someone will be coming from the Administrator's office to look over his papers and effects before communicating with the next of kin—all that sort of thing—If you could describe this snapshot.'

'It was just the front of a house,' said Miss Marple. 'And someone—Denzil, I mean—was just coming out of the front door. As I say it was taken by one of my other nephews who is very keen on flower shows—and he was photographing a hibiscus, I think, or one of those beautiful—something like antipasto—lilies. Denzil just happened to come out of the front door at that time. It wasn't a very good photograph of him—just a trifle blurred—But I liked it and have always kept it.'

'Well,' said Dr Graham, 'that seems clear enough. I think we'll have no difficulty in getting back your picture for you, Miss Marple.'

He rose from his chair. Miss Marple smiled up at him.

'You are very kind, Dr Graham, very kind *indeed*. You do understand, don't you?'

'Of course I do, of course I do,' said Dr Graham, shaking her warmly by the hand. 'Now don't you worry. Exercise that knee every day gently but not too much, and I'll send you round these tablets. Take one three times a day.'

CHAPTER 5

Miss Marple Makes a Decision

The funeral service was said over the body of the late Major Palgrave on the following day. Miss Marple attended in company with Miss Prescott. The Canon read the service—after that life went on as usual.

Major Palgrave's death was already only an incident, a slightly unpleasant incident, but one that was soon forgotten. Life here was sunshine, sea, and social pleasures. A grim visitor had interrupted these activities, casting a momentary shadow, but the shadow was now gone. After all, nobody had known the deceased very well. He had been rather a garrulous elderly man of the club-bore type, always telling you personal reminiscences that you had no particular desire to hear. He had had little to anchor himself to any particular part of the world. His wife had died many years ago. He had had a lonely life and a lonely death. But it had been the kind of loneliness that spends itself in living amongst people, and in passing the time that way not unpleasantly. Major Palgrave might have been a lonely man, he had also been quite a cheerful one. He had enjoyed himself in his own particular way. And now he was dead, buried, and nobody cared very much, and in another week's time nobody would even remember him or spare him a passing thought.

The only person who could possibly be said to miss him was Miss Marple. Not indeed out of any personal affection, but he represented a kind of life that she knew. As one grew older, so she reflected to herself, one got more and more into the habit of listening; listening possibly without any great interest, but there had been between her and the Major the gentle give and take of two old people. It had had a cheerful, human quality. She did not actually mourn Major Palgrave but she missed him.

On the afternoon of the funeral, as she was sitting knitting in her favourite spot, Dr Graham came and joined her. She put her needles down and greeted him. He said at once, rather apologetically:

'I am afraid I have rather disappointing news, Miss Marple.'

'Indeed? About my—'

'Yes. We haven't found that precious snapshot of yours. I'm afraid that will be a disappointment to you.'

'Yes. Yes it is. But of course it does not *really* matter. It was a sentimentality. I do realize that now. It wasn't in Major Palgrave's wallet?'

'No. Nor anywhere else among his things. There were a few letters and newspaper clippings and odds and ends, and a few old photographs, but no sign of a snapshot such as you mentioned.'

'Oh dear,' said Miss Marple. 'Well, it can't be helped . . . Thank you very much, Dr Graham, for the trouble you've taken.'

'Oh it was no trouble, indeed. But I know quite well from my own experience how much family trifles mean to one, especially as one is getting older.'

The old lady was really taking it very well, he thought. Major Palgrave, he presumed, had probably come across the snapshot when taking something out of his wallet, and not even realizing how it had come there, had torn it up as something of no importance. But of course it was of great importance to this old lady. Still, she seemed quite cheerful and philosophical about it.

Internally, however, Miss Marple was far from being either cheerful or philosophical. She wanted a little time in which to think things out, but she was also determined to use her present opportunities to the fullest effect.

She engaged Dr Graham in conversation with an eagerness which she did not attempt to conceal. That kindly man, putting down her flow of talk to the natural loneliness of an old lady, exerted himself to divert her mind from the loss of the snapshot, by conversing easily and pleasantly about life in St Honoré, and the various interesting places perhaps Miss Marple might like to visit. He hardly knew himself how the conversation drifted back to Major Palgrave's decease.

'It seems so sad,' said Miss Marple. 'To think of anyone dying like this away from home. Though I gather, from what he himself told me, that he had no immediate family. It seems he lived by himself in London.'

'He travelled a fair amount, I believe,' said Dr Graham. 'At any rate in the winters. He didn't care for our English winters. Can't say I blame him.'

'No, indeed,' said Miss Marple. 'And perhaps he had some special reason like a weakness of the lungs or something which made it necessary for him to winter abroad?'

'Oh no, I don't think so.'

'He had high blood pressure, I believe. So sad nowadays. One hears so much of it.'

'He spoke about it to you, did he?'

'Oh no. No, *he* never mentioned it. It was somebody else who told me.'

'Ah, really.'

'I suppose,' went on Miss Marple, 'that death was to be expected under those circumstances.'

'Not necessarily,' said Dr Graham. 'There are methods of controlling blood pressure nowadays.'

'His death *seemed* very sudden—but I suppose *you* weren't surprised.'

'Well I wasn't particularly surprised in a man of that age. But I certainly didn't expect it. Frankly, he always seemed to me in very good form, but I hadn't ever attended him professionally. I'd never taken his blood pressure or anything like that.'

'Does one know—I mean, does a doctor know—when a man has high blood pressure just by looking at him?' Miss Marple inquired with a kind of dewy innocence.

'Not just by looking,' said the doctor, smiling. 'One has to do a bit of testing.'

'Oh I see. That dreadful thing when you put a rubber band round somebody's arm and blow it up—I dislike it *so* much. But my doctor said that my blood pressure was really very good for my age.'

'Well, that's good hearing,' said Dr Graham.

'Of course, the Major *was* rather fond of Planters Punch,' said Miss Marple thoughtfully.

'Yes. Not the best thing with blood pressure—alcohol.'

'One takes tablets, doesn't one, or so I have heard?'

'Yes. There are several on the market. There was a bottle of one of them in his room—Serenite.'

'How wonderful science is nowadays,' said Miss Marple. 'Doctors can do so much, can't they?'

'We all have one great competitor,' said Dr Graham. 'Nature, you know. And some of the good old-fashioned home remedies come back from time to time.'

'Like putting cobwebs on a cut?' said Miss Marple. 'We always used to do that when I was a child.'

'Very sensible,' said Dr Graham.

'And a linseed poultice on the chest and rubbing in camphorated oil for a bad cough.'

'I see you know it all!' said Dr Graham laughing. He got up. 'How's the knee? Not been too troublesome?'

'No, it seems much, much better.'

'Well, we won't say whether that's Nature or my pills,' said Dr Graham. 'Sorry I couldn't have been of more help to you.'

'But you have been most kind—I am really ashamed of taking up your time—Did you say that there were no photographs in the Major's wallet?'

'Oh yes—a very old one of the Major himself as quite a young man on a polo pony—and one of a dead tiger— He was standing with his foot on it. Snaps of that sort—memories of his younger days—But I looked very carefully, I assure you, and the one you describe of your nephew was definitely not there—'

'Oh I'm sure you looked carefully—I didn't mean that—I was just interested—We all tend to keep such very odd things—'

'Treasures from the past,' said the doctor smiling.

He said goodbye and departed.

Miss Marple remained looking thoughtfully at the palm trees and the sea. She did not pick up her knitting again for some minutes. She had a fact now. She had to think about that fact and what it meant. The snapshot that the Major had brought out of his wallet and replaced so hurriedly was *not there after he died*. It was not the sort of thing the Major would throw away. He had replaced it in his wallet and it ought to have been in his wallet after his death. Money might have been stolen, but no one would want to steal a snapshot. Unless, that is, they had a special reason for so doing . . .

Miss Marple's face was grave. She had to take a decision. Was she, or was she not, going to allow Major Palgrave to remain quietly in his grave? Might it not be better to do just that? She quoted under her breath. 'Duncan is dead. After Life's fitful fever he sleeps well!' Nothing could hurt Major Palgrave now. He had gone where danger could not touch him. Was it just a coincidence that he should have died on that particular night?

Or was it just possibly *not* a coincidence? Doctors accepted the deaths of elderly men so easily. Especially since in his room there had been a bottle of the tablets that people with high blood pressure had to take every day of their lives. But if someone had taken the snapshot from the Major's wallet, that same person could have put that bottle of tablets in the Major's room. She herself never remembered *seeing* the Major take tablets; he had never spoken about his blood pressure to her. The only thing he had ever said about his health was the admission—'Not as young as I was.' He had been occasionally a little short of breath, a trifle asthmatic, nothing else. But someone had mentioned that Major Palgrave had high blood pressure—Molly? Miss Prescott? She couldn't remember.

Miss Marple sighed, then admonished herself in words, though she did not speak those words aloud.

'Now, Jane, what are you suggesting or thinking? Are you, perhaps, just making the whole thing up? Have you *really* got anything to build on?'

She went over, step by step, as nearly as she could, the conversation between herself and the Major on the subject of murder and murderers.

'Oh dear,' said Miss Marple. 'Even if—really, I *don't* see how I *can* do anything about it—'

But she knew that she meant to try.

CHAPTER 6

In the Small Hours

Miss Marple woke early. Like many old people she slept
lightly and had periods of wakefulness which she used for
the planning of some action or actions to be carried out
on the next or following days. Usually, of course, these
were of a wholly private or domestic nature, of little interest
to anybody but herself. But this morning Miss Marple lay
thinking soberly and constructively of murder, and what,
if her suspicions were correct, she could do about it. It
wasn't going to be easy. She had one weapon and one
weapon only, and that was conversation.

Old ladies were given to a good deal of rambling
conversation. People were bored by this, but certainly did
not suspect them of ulterior motives. It would not be a
case of asking direct questions. (Indeed, she would have
found it difficult to know what questions to ask!) It would
be a question of finding out a little more about certain
people. She reviewed these certain people in her mind.

She could find out, possibly, a little more about Major
Palgrave, but would that really help her? She doubted if

it would. If Major Palgrave had been killed it was not because of secrets in his life or to inherit his money or for revenge upon him. In fact, although he was the victim, it was one of those rare cases where a greater knowledge of the victim does not help you or lead you in any way to his murderer. The point, it seemed to her, and the sole point, was that Major Palgrave talked too much!

She had learnt one rather interesting fact from Dr Graham. He had had in his wallet various photographs: one of himself in company with a polo pony, one of a dead tiger, also one or two other shots of the same nature. Now why did Major Palgrave carry these about with him? Obviously, thought Miss Marple, with long experience of old admirals, brigadier-generals and mere majors behind her, because he had certain stories which he enjoyed telling to people. Starting off with 'Curious thing happened once when I was out tiger shooting in India . . .' Or a reminiscence of himself and a polo pony. Therefore this story about a suspected murderer would in due course be illustrated by the production of the snapshot from his wallet.

He had been following that pattern in his conversation with her. The subject of murder having come up, and to focus interest on his story, he had done what he no doubt usually did, produced his snapshot and said something in the nature of 'Wouldn't think this chap was a murderer, would you?'

The point was that it had been a *habit* of his. This murderer story was one of his regular repertoire. If any reference to murder came up, then away went the Major, full steam ahead.

In that case, reflected Miss Marple, he might *already* have told his story to someone else here. Or to more than one person—If that were so, then she herself might learn from that person what the further details of the story had been, possibly what the person in the snapshot had looked like.

She nodded her head in satisfaction—That would be a beginning.

And, of course, there were the people she called in her mind the 'Four Suspects'. Though really, since Major Palgrave had been talking about a *man*—there were only two. Colonel Hillingdon or Mr Dyson, very unlikely-looking murderers, but then murderers so often *were* unlikely. Could there have been anyone else? She had seen no one when she turned her head to look. There was the bungalow of course. Mr Rafiel's bungalow. Could somebody have come out of the bungalow and gone in again before she had had time to turn her head? If so, it could only have been the valet-attendant. What was his name? Oh yes, Jackson. Could it have been *Jackson* who had come out of the door? That would have been the same pose as the photograph. *A man coming out of a door*. Recognition might have struck suddenly. Up till then, Major Palgrave would not have looked at Arthur Jackson, valet-attendant, with any interest. His roving and curious eye was essentially a snobbish eye— Arthur Jackson was not a *pukka sahib*—Major Palgrave would not have glanced at him twice.

Until, perhaps, he had had the snapshot in his hand, and had looked over Miss Marple's right shoulder and had seen a man coming out of a door . . .?

Miss Marple turned over on her pillow—Programme for tomorrow—or rather for today—Further investigation of the Hillingdons, the Dysons and Arthur Jackson, valet-attendant.

Dr Graham also woke early. Usually he turned over and went to sleep again. But today he was uneasy and sleep failed to come. This anxiety that made it so difficult to go to sleep again was a thing he had not suffered from for a long time. What was causing this anxiety? Really, he couldn't make it out. He lay there thinking it over. Something to do with—something to do with—yes, Major Palgrave. Major Palgrave's death? He didn't see, though, what there could be to make him uneasy there. Was it something that that twittery old lady had said? Bad luck for her about her snapshot. She'd taken it very well. But now what was it she had said, what chance word of hers had it been, that had given him this funny feeling of uneasiness? After all, there was nothing *odd* about the Major's death. Nothing at all. At least he supposed there was nothing at all.

It was quite clear that in the Major's state of health— a faint check came in his thought process. Did he really know much *about* Major Palgrave's state of health? Everybody *said* that he'd suffered from high blood pressure. But he himself had never had any conversation with the Major about it. But then he'd never had much conversation with Major Palgrave anyway. Palgrave was an old bore and he avoided old bores. Why on earth should he have this idea that perhaps everything *mightn't* be all right? Was it that old woman? But after all she hadn't *said* anything. Anyway, it was none of his business. The local authorities were quite satisfied. There had been that bottle of Serenite tablets, and the old boy had apparently talked to people about his blood pressure quite freely.

Dr Graham turned over in bed and soon went to sleep again.

Outside the hotel grounds, in one of a row of shanty cabins beside a creek, the girl Victoria Johnson rolled over and sat up in bed. The St Honoré girl was a magnificent creature with a torso of black marble such as a sculptor would have enjoyed. She ran her fingers through her dark, tightly curling hair. With her foot she nudged her sleeping companion in the ribs.

'Wake up, man.'

The man grunted and turned.

'What you want? It's not morning.'

'Wake up, man. I want to talk to you.'

The man sat up, stretched, showed a wide mouth and beautiful teeth.

'What's worrying you, woman?'

'That Major man who died. Something I don't like. Something wrong about it.'

'Ah, what d'you want to worry about that? He was old. He died.'

'Listen, man. It's them pills. Them pills the doctor asked me about.'

'Well, what about them? He took too many maybe.'

'No. It's not that. Listen.' She leant towards him, talking vehemently. He yawned and lay down again.

'There's nothing in that. What're you talking about?'

'All the same, I'll speak to Mrs Kendal about it in the morning. I think there's something wrong there somewhere.'

'Shouldn't bother,' said the man who, without benefit of ceremony, she considered as her present husband. 'Don't let's look for trouble,' he said and rolled over on his side yawning.

CHAPTER 7

Morning on the Beach

It was mid-morning on the beach below the hotel.

Evelyn Hillingdon came out of the water and dropped on the warm golden sand. She took off her bathing cap and shook her dark head vigorously. The beach was not a very big one. People tended to congregate there in the mornings and about 11.30 there was always something of a social reunion. To Evelyn's left in one of the exotic-looking modern basket chairs lay Señora de Caspearo, a handsome woman from Venezuela. Next to her was old Mr Rafiel who was by now the doyen of the Golden Palm Hotel and held the sway that only an elderly invalid of great wealth could attain. Esther Walters was in attendance on him. She usually had her shorthand notebook and pencil with her in case Mr Rafiel should suddenly think of urgent business cables which must be got off at once. Mr Rafiel in beach attire was incredibly desiccated, his bones draped with festoons of dry skin. Though looking like a man on the point of death, he had looked exactly the same for at least the last eight years—or so it was said in the islands. Sharp blue eyes peered out of his wrinkled cheeks, and his principal pleasure in life was denying robustly anything that anyone else said.

Miss Marple was also present. As usual she sat and knitted and listened to what went on, and very occasionally joined in the conversation. When she did so, everyone was surprised because they had usually forgotten that she was there! Evelyn Hillingdon looked at her indulgently, and thought that she was a nice old pussy.

Señora de Caspearo rubbed some more oil on her long beautiful legs and hummed to herself. She was not a woman who spoke much. She looked discontentedly at the flask of sun oil.

'This is not so good as Frangipanio,' she said, sadly. 'One cannot get it here. A pity.' Her eyelids drooped again.

'Are you going in for your dip now, Mr Rafiel?' asked Esther Walters.

'I'll go in when I'm ready,' said Mr Rafiel, snappishly.

'It's half past eleven,' said Mrs Walters.

'What of it?' said Mr Rafiel. 'Think I'm the kind of man to be tied by the clock? Do this at the hour, do this at twenty minutes past, do that at twenty to—bah!'

Mrs Walters had been in attendance on Mr Rafiel long enough to have adopted her own formula for dealing with him. She knew that he liked a good space of time in which to recover from the exertion of bathing and she had therefore reminded him of the time, allowing a good ten minutes for him to rebut her suggestion and then be able to adopt it without seeming to do so.

'I don't like these espadrilles,' said Mr Rafiel, raising a foot and looking at it. 'I told that fool Jackson so. The man never pays attention to a word I say.'

'I'll fetch you some others, shall I, Mr Rafiel?'

'No, you won't, you'll sit here and keep quiet. I hate people rushing about like clucking hens.'

Evelyn shifted slightly in the warm sand, stretching out her arms.

Miss Marple, intent on her knitting—or so it seemed—stretched out a foot, then hastily she apologized.

'I'm so sorry, so very sorry, Mrs Hillingdon. I'm afraid I kicked you.'

'Oh, it's quite all right,' said Evelyn. 'This beach gets rather crowded.'

'Oh, please don't move. Please. I'll move my chair a little back so that I won't do it again.'

As Miss Marple resettled herself, she went on talking in a childish and garrulous manner.

'It still seems so wonderful to be *here*! I've never been to the West Indies before, you know. I thought it was the kind of place I never should come to and here I am. All by the kindness of my dear nephew. I suppose you know this part of the world very well, don't you, Mrs Hillingdon?'

'I have been in this island once or twice before and of course in most of the others.'

'Oh yes. Butterflies isn't it, and wild flowers? You and your—your friends—or are they relations?'

'Friends. Nothing more.'

'And I suppose you go about together a great deal because of your interests being the same?'

'Yes. We've travelled together for some years now.'

'I suppose you must have had some rather exciting adventures sometimes?'

'I don't think so,' said Evelyn. Her voice was unaccentuated, slightly bored. 'Adventures always seem to happen to other people.' She yawned.

'No dangerous encounters with snakes or with wild animals or with natives gone berserk?'

('What a fool I sound,' thought Miss Marple.)

'Nothing worse than insect bites,' Evelyn assured her.

'Poor Major Palgrave, you know, was bitten by a snake once,' said Miss Marple, making a purely fictitious statement.

'Was he?'

'Did he never tell you about it?'

'Perhaps. I don't remember.'

'I suppose you knew him quite well, didn't you?'

'Major Palgrave? No, hardly at all.'

'He always had so many interesting stories to tell.'

'Ghastly old bore,' said Mr Rafiel. 'Silly fool, too. He needn't have died if he'd looked after himself properly.'

'Oh come now, Mr Rafiel,' said Mrs Walters.

'I know what I'm talking about. If you look after your health properly you're all right anywhere. Look at me. The doctors gave *me* up years ago. All right, I said, I've got my own rules of health and I shall keep to them. And here I am.'

He looked round proudly.

It did indeed seem rather a mistake that he should be there.

'Poor Major Palgrave had high blood pressure,' said Mrs Walters.

'Nonsense,' said Mr Rafiel.

'Oh, but he did,' said Evelyn Hillingdon. She spoke with sudden, unexpected authority.

'Who says so?' said Mr Rafiel. 'Did he tell you so?'

'Somebody said so.'

'He looked very red in the face,' Miss Marple contributed.

'Can't go by that,' said Mr Rafiel. 'And anyway he *didn't* have high blood pressure because he told me so.'

'What do you mean, he told you so?' said Mrs Walters. 'I mean, you can't exactly tell people you *haven't* got a thing.'

'Yes you can. I said to him once when he was downing all those Planters Punches, and eating too much, I said, "You ought to watch your diet and your drink. You've got to think of your blood pressure at your age." And he said he'd nothing to look out for in that line, that his blood pressure was very good for his age.'

'But he took some stuff for it, I believe,' said Miss Marple, entering the conversation once more. 'Some stuff called—oh, something like—was it Serenite?'

'If you ask me,' said Evelyn Hillingdon, 'I don't think he ever liked to admit that there could be anything the matter with him or that he could be ill. I think he was one of those people who are afraid of illness and therefore deny there's ever anything wrong with them.'

It was a long speech for her. Miss Marple looked thoughtfully down at the top of her dark head.

'The trouble is,' said Mr Rafiel dictatorially, 'everybody's too fond of knowing other people's ailments. They think everybody over fifty is going to die of hypertension or coronary thrombosis or one of those things—poppycock! If a man says there's nothing much wrong with him I don't suppose there is. A man ought to know about his own health. What's the time? Quarter to twelve? I ought to have had my dip long ago. Why can't you remind me about these things, Esther?'

Mrs Walters made no protest. She rose to her feet and with some deftness assisted Mr Rafiel to his. Together they went down the beach, she supporting him carefully. Together they stepped into the sea.

Señora de Caspearo opened her eyes and murmured: 'How ugly are old men! Oh how they are ugly! They should all be put to death at forty, or perhaps thirty-five would be better. Yes?'

Edward Hillingdon and Gregory Dyson came crunching down the beach.

'What's the water like, Evelyn?'

'Just the same as always.'

'Never much variation, is there? Where's Lucky?'

'I don't know,' said Evelyn.

Again Miss Marple looked down thoughtfully at the dark head.

'Well, now I give my imitation of a whale,' said Gregory. He threw off his gaily patterned Bermuda shirt and tore down the beach, flinging himself, puffing and panting, into the sea, doing a fast crawl. Edward Hillingdon sat down on the beach by his wife. Presently he asked, 'Coming in again?'

She smiled—put on her cap—and they went down the beach together in a much less spectacular manner.

Señora de Caspearo opened her eyes again.

'I think at first those two they are on their honeymoon, he is so charming to her, but I hear they have been married eight—nine years. It is incredible, is it not?'

'I wonder where Mrs Dyson is?' said Miss Marple.

'That Lucky? She is with some man.'

'You—you think so?'

'It is certain,' said Señora de Caspearo. 'She is that type. But she is not so young any longer—Her husband—already his eyes go elsewhere—He makes passes—here, there, all the time. I know.'

'Yes,' said Miss Marple. 'I expect you would know.'

Señora de Caspearo shot a surprised glance at her. It was clearly not what she had expected from that quarter.

Miss Marple, however, was looking at the waves with an air of gentle innocence.

'May I speak to you, ma'am, Mrs Kendal?'

'Yes, of course,' said Molly. She was sitting at her desk in the office.

Victoria Johnson, tall and buoyant in her crisp white uniform, came in farther and shut the door behind her with a somewhat mysterious air.

'I like to tell you something, please, Mrs Kendal.'

'Yes, what is it? Is anything wrong?'

'I don't know that. Not for sure. It's the old gentleman who died. The Major gentleman. He die in his sleep.'

'Yes, yes. What about it?'

'There was a bottle of pills in his room. Doctor, he asked me about them.'

'Yes?'

'The doctor said—"Let me see what he has here on the bathroom shelf," and he looked, you see. He see there was tooth powder and indigestion pills and aspirin and cascara pills, and then these pills in a bottle called Serenite.'

'Yes,' repeated Molly yet again.

'And the doctor looked at them. He seemed quite satisfied, and nodded his head. But I get to thinking afterwards. Those pills weren't there before. I've not seen them in his bathroom before. The others, yes. The tooth powder and the aspirin and the aftershave lotion and all the rest. But those pills, those Serenite pills, I never noticed them before.'

'So you think—' Molly looked puzzled.

'I don't know what to think,' said Victoria. 'I just think it's not right, so I think I better tell you about it. Perhaps you tell doctor? Perhaps it means something. Perhaps *someone* put those pills there so he take them and he died.'

'Oh, I don't think that's likely at all,' said Molly.

Victoria shook her dark head. 'You never know. People do bad things.'

Molly glanced out of the window. The place looked like an earthly paradise. With its sunshine, its sea, its coral reef, its music, its dancing, it seemed a Garden of Eden. But even in the Garden of Eden, there had been a shadow—the shadow of the Serpent—*Bad things*—how hateful to hear those words.

'I'll make inquiries, Victoria,' she said sharply. 'Don't worry. And above all don't go starting a lot of silly rumours.'

Tim Kendal came in, just as Victoria was, somewhat unwillingly, leaving.

'Anything wrong, Molly?'

She hesitated—but Victoria might go to him—She told him what the girl had said.

'I don't see what all this rigmarole—what *were* these pills anyway?'

'Well, I don't really know, Tim. Dr Robertson when he came said they—were something to do with blood pressure, I think.'

'Well, that would be all right, wouldn't it? I mean, he *had* high blood pressure, and he *would* be taking things for it, wouldn't he? People do. I've seen them, lots of times.'

'Yes,' Molly hesitated, 'but Victoria seemed to think that he might have taken one of these pills and it would have killed him.'

'Oh darling, that is a bit *too* melodramatic! You mean that somebody might have changed his blood pressure pills for something else, and that they poisoned him?'

'It does sound absurd,' said Molly apologetically, 'when you say it like that. But that seemed to be what Victoria thought!'

'Silly girl! We *could* go and ask Dr Graham about it,

I suppose he'd know. But really it's such nonsense that it's not worth bothering him.'

'That's what I think.'

'What on earth made the girl think anybody would have changed the pills? You mean, put different pills into the same bottle?'

'I didn't quite gather,' said Molly, looking rather helpless. 'Victoria seemed to think that was the first time that Serenite bottle had been there.'

'Oh but that's nonsense,' said Tim Kendal. 'He had to take those pills all the time to keep his blood pressure down.' And he went off cheerfully to consult with Fernando the *maître d'hôtel*.

But Molly could not dismiss the matter so lightly. After the stress of lunch was over she said to her husband:

'Tim—I've been thinking—If Victoria is going around talking about this perhaps we ought just to ask someone about it?'

'My dear girl! Robertson and all the rest of them came and looked at everything and asked all the questions they wanted at the time.'

'Yes, but you know how they work themselves up, these girls—'

'Oh, all right! I'll tell you what—we'll go and ask Graham—he'll know.'

Dr Graham was sitting on his loggia with a book. The young couple came in and Molly plunged into her recital. It was a little incoherent and Tim took over.

'Sounds rather idiotic,' he said apologetically, 'but as far as I can make out, this girl has got it into her head that someone put some poison tablets in the—what's the name of the stuff—Sera—something bottle.'

'But why should she get this idea into her head?' asked Dr Graham. 'Did she see anything or hear anything or—I mean, why should she think so?'

'I don't know,' said Tim rather helplessly. 'Was it a different bottle? Was that it, Molly?'

'No,' said Molly. 'I think what she said was that there was a bottle there labelled—Seven—Seren—'

'Serenite,' said the doctor. 'That's quite right. A well-known preparation. He'd been taking it regularly.'

'Victoria said she'd never seen it in his room before.'

'Never seen it in his room before?' said Graham sharply. 'What does she mean by that?'

'Well, that's what she *said*. She said there were all sorts of things on the bathroom shelf. You know, tooth powder, aspirin and aftershave and—oh—she rattled them off gaily. I suppose she's always cleaning them and so she knows them all off by heart. But this one—the Serenite—she hadn't seen it there until the day after he died.'

'That's very odd,' said Dr Graham, rather sharply. 'Is she sure?'

The unusual sharpness of his tone made both of the Kendals look up at him. They had not expected Dr Graham to take up quite this attitude.

'She sounded sure,' said Molly slowly.

'Perhaps she just wanted to be sensational,' suggested Tim.

'I think perhaps,' said Dr Graham, 'I'd better have a few words with the girl myself.'

Victoria displayed a distinct pleasure at being allowed to tell her story.

'I don't want to get in no trouble,' she said. '*I* didn't put that bottle there and I don't know who did.'

'But you think it *was* put there?' asked Graham.

'Well, you see, Doctor, it *must* have been put there if it wasn't there before.'

'Major Palgrave could have kept it in a drawer—or a dispatch-case, something like that.'

Victoria shook her head shrewdly.

'Wouldn't do that if he was taking it all the time, would he?'

'No,' said Graham reluctantly. 'No, it was stuff he would have to take several times a day. You never saw him taking it or anything of that kind?'

'He didn't have it there before. I just thought—word got round as that stuff had something to do with his death, poisoned his blood or something, and I thought maybe he had an enemy put it there so as to kill him.'

'Nonsense, my girl,' said the doctor robustly. 'Sheer nonsense.'

Victoria looked shaken.

'You say as this stuff was medicine, good medicine?' she asked doubtfully.

'Good medicine, and what is more, *necessary* medicine,' said Dr Graham. 'So you needn't worry, Victoria. I can assure you there was nothing wrong with that medicine.

It was the proper thing for a man to take who had his complaint.'

'Surely you've taken a load off my mind,' said Victoria. She showed white teeth at him in a cheerful smile.

But the load was not taken off Dr Graham's mind. That uneasiness of his that had been so nebulous was now becoming tangible.

CHAPTER 8

A Talk with Esther Walters

'This place isn't what it used to be,' said Mr Rafiel, irritably, as he observed Miss Marple approaching the spot where he and his secretary were sitting. 'Can't move a step without some old hen getting under your feet. What do old ladies want to come to the West Indies for?'

'Where do you suggest they should go?' asked Esther Walters.

'To Cheltenham,' said Mr Rafiel promptly. 'Or Bournemouth,' he offered, 'or Torquay or Llandrindod Wells. Plenty of choice. They like it there—they're quite happy.'

'They can't often afford to come to the West Indies, I suppose,' said Esther. 'It isn't everyone who is as lucky as you are.'

'That's right,' said Mr Rafiel. 'Rub it in. Here am I, a mass of aches and pains and disjoints. You grudge me any alleviation! And you don't do any work—Why haven't you typed out those letters yet?'

'I haven't had time.'

'Well, get on with it, can't you? I bring you out here

61

to do a bit of work, not to sit about sunning yourself and showing off your figure.'

Some people would have considered Mr Rafiel's remarks quite insupportable but Esther Walters had worked for him for some years and she knew well enough that Mr Rafiel's bark was a great deal worse than his bite. He was a man who suffered almost continual pain, and making disagreeable remarks was one of his ways of letting off steam. No matter what he said she remained quite imperturbable.

'Such a lovely evening, isn't it?' said Miss Marple, pausing beside them.

'Why not?' said Mr Rafiel. 'That's what we're here for, isn't it?'

Miss Marple gave a tinkly little laugh.

'You're so severe—of course the weather *is* a very English subject of conversation—one forgets—Oh dear—this is the wrong coloured wool.' She deposited her knitting bag on the garden table and trotted towards her own bungalow.

'Jackson!' yelled Mr Rafiel.

Jackson appeared.

'Take me back inside,' said Mr Rafiel. 'I'll have my massage now before that chattering hen comes back. Not that massage does me a bit of good,' he added. Having said which, he allowed himself to be deftly helped to his feet and went off with the masseur beside him into his bungalow.

Esther Walters looked after them and then turned her head as Miss Marple came back with a ball of wool to sit down near her.

'I hope I'm not disturbing you?' said Miss Marple.

'Of course not,' said Esther Walters, 'I've got to go off and do some typing in a minute, but I'm going to enjoy another ten minutes of the sunset first.'

Miss Marple sat down and in a gentle voice began to talk. As she talked, she summed up Esther Walters. Not at all glamorous, but could be attractive-looking if she tried. Miss Marple wondered why she didn't try. It could be, of course, because Mr Rafiel would not have liked it, but Miss Marple didn't think Mr Rafiel would really mind in the least. He was so completely taken up with himself that so long as he was not personally neglected, his secretary might have got herself up like a houri in Paradise without his objecting. Besides, he usually went to bed early and in the evening hours of steel bands and dancing, Esther Walters might easily have—Miss Marple paused to select a word in her mind, at the same time conversing cheerfully about her visit to Jamestown—Ah yes, *blossomed*. Esther Walters might have blossomed in the evening hours.

She led the conversation gently in the direction of Jackson.

On the subject of Jackson Esther Walters was rather vague.

'He's very competent,' she said. 'A fully trained masseur.'

'I suppose he's been with Mr Rafiel a long time?'

'Oh no—about nine months, I think—'

'Is he married?' Miss Marple hazarded.

'Married? I don't think so,' said Esther, slightly surprised. 'He's never mentioned it if so—

'No,' she added. 'Definitely *not* married, I should say.' And she showed amusement.

Miss Marple interpreted that by adding to it in her own mind the following sentence—'At any rate he doesn't behave as though he were married.'

But then, how many married men there were who behaved as though they weren't married! Miss Marple could think of a dozen examples!

'He's quite good-looking,' she said thoughtfully.

'Yes—I suppose he is,' said Esther without interest.

Miss Marple considered her thoughtfully. Uninterested in men? The kind of woman, perhaps, who was only interested in one man—A widow, they had said.

She asked—'Have you worked for Mr Rafiel long?'

'Four or five years. After my husband died, I had to take a job again. I've got a daughter at school and my husband left me very badly off.'

'Mr Rafiel must be a difficult man to work for?' Miss Marple hazarded.

'Not really, when you get to know him. He flies into rages and is very contradictory. I think the real trouble is he gets tired of people. He's had five different valet-attendants in two years. He likes having someone new to bully. But he and I have always got on very well.'

'Mr Jackson seems a very obliging young man?'

'He's very tactful and resourceful,' said Esther. 'Of course, he's sometimes a little—' She broke off.

Miss Marple considered. 'Rather a difficult position sometimes?' she suggested.

'Well, yes. Neither one thing nor the other. However—'

she smiled—'I think he manages to have quite a good time.'

Miss Marple considered this also. It didn't help her much. She continued her twittering conversation and soon she was hearing a good deal about that nature-loving quartet, the Dysons and the Hillingdons.

'The Hillingdons have been here for the last three or four years at least,' said Esther, 'but Gregory Dyson has been here much longer than that. He knows the West Indies very well. He came here, originally, I believe, with his first wife. She was delicate and had to go abroad in the winters, or go somewhere warm, at any rate.'

'And she died? Or was it divorce?'

'No. She died. Out here, I believe. I don't mean this particular island but one of the West Indies islands. There was some sort of trouble, I believe, some kind of scandal or other. He never talks about her. Somebody else told me about it. They didn't, I gather, get on very well together.'

'And then he married this wife. "Lucky".' Miss Marple said the word with faint dissatisfaction as if to say 'Really, a most incredible name!'

'I believe she was a relation of his first wife.'

'Have they known the Hillingdons a great many years?'

'Oh, I think only since the Hillingdons came out here. Three or four years, not more.'

'The Hillingdons seem very pleasant,' said Miss Marple. 'Quiet, of course.'

'Yes. They're both quiet.'

'Everyone says they're very devoted to each other,' said

Agatha Christie

Miss Marple. The tone of her voice was quite non-committal but Esther Walters looked at her sharply.

'But you don't think they are?' she said.

'You don't really think so yourself, do you, my dear?'

'Well, I've wondered sometimes . . .'

'Quiet men, like Colonel Hillingdon,' said Miss Marple, 'are often attracted to flamboyant types.' And she added, after a significant pause, 'Lucky—such a curious name. Do you think Mr Dyson has any idea of—of what might be going on?'

'Old scandal-monger,' thought Esther Walters. 'Really, these old women!'

She said rather coldly, 'I've no idea.'

Miss Marple shifted to another subject. 'It's very sad about poor Major Palgrave, isn't it?' she said.

Esther Walters agreed, though in a somewhat perfunctory fashion.

'The people I'm really sorry for are the Kendals,' she said.

'Yes, I suppose it is really rather unfortunate when something of that kind happens in a hotel.'

'People come here, you see, to enjoy themselves, don't they?' said Esther. 'To forget about illnesses and deaths and income tax and frozen pipes and all the rest of it. They don't like—' she went on, with a sudden flash of an entirely different manner—'any reminders of mortality.'

Miss Marple laid down her knitting. 'Now that is very well put, my dear,' she said, 'very well put indeed. Yes, it is as you say.'

'And you see they're quite a young couple,' went on Esther Walters. 'They only just took over from the

Sandersons six months ago and they're terribly worried about whether they're going to succeed or not, because they haven't had much experience.'

'And you think this might be really disadvantageous to them?'

'Well, no, I don't, frankly,' said Esther Walters. 'I don't think people remember anything for more than a day or two, not in this atmosphere of "we've-all-come-out-here-to-enjoy-ourselves-let's-get-on-with-it". I think a death just gives them a jolt for about twenty-four hours or so and then they don't think of it again once the funeral is over. Not unless they're reminded of it, that is. I've told Molly so, but of course she is a worrier.'

'Mrs Kendal is a worrier? She always seems so carefree.'

'I think a lot of that is put on,' said Esther slowly. 'Actually, I think she's one of those anxious sort of people who can't help worrying all the time that things *may* go wrong.'

'I should have thought *he* worried more than she did.'

'No, I don't think so. I think she's the worrier and he worries because she worries if you know what I mean.'

'That is interesting,' said Miss Marple.

'I think Molly wants desperately to try and appear very gay and to be enjoying herself. She works at it very hard but the effort exhausts her. Then she has these odd fits of depression. She's not—well, not really well-balanced.'

'Poor child,' said Miss Marple. 'There certainly are people like that, and very often outsiders don't suspect it.'

'No, they put on such a good show, don't they? However,' Esther added, 'I don't think Molly has really anything to worry about in this case. I mean, people are dying of coronary thrombosis or cerebral h'morrhage or things of that kind all the time nowadays. Far more than they used to, as far as I can see. It's only food poisoning or typhoid or something like that, that makes people get het up.'

'Major Palgrave never mentioned to *me* that he had high blood pressure,' said Miss Marple. 'Did he to you?'

'He said so to somebody—I don't know who—it may have been to Mr Rafiel. I know Mr Rafiel says just the opposite—but then he's like that! Certainly Jackson mentioned it to me once. He said the Major ought to be more careful over the alcohol he took.'

'I see,' said Miss Marple, thoughtfully. She went on: 'I expect you found him rather a boring old man? He told a lot of stories and I expect repeated himself a good deal.'

'That's the worst of it,' said Esther. 'You do hear the same story again and again unless you can manage to be quick enough to fend it off.'

'Of course *I* didn't mind so much,' said Miss Marple, 'because I'm used to that sort of thing. If I get stories told to me rather often, I don't really mind hearing them again because I've usually forgotten them.'

'There is that,' said Esther and laughed cheerfully.

'There was one story he was very fond of telling,' said Miss Marple, 'about a murder. I expect he told you that, didn't he?'

Esther Walters opened her handbag and started searching through it. She drew out her lipstick saying, 'I thought I'd lost it.' Then she asked, 'I beg your pardon, what did you say?'

'I asked if Major Palgrave told you his favourite murder story?'

'I believe he did, now I come to think of it. Something about someone who gassed themselves, wasn't it? Only really it was the *wife* who gassed him. I mean she'd given him a sedative of some kind and then stuck his head in the gas oven. Was that it?'

'I don't think that was exactly it,' said Miss Marple. She looked at Esther Walters thoughtfully.

'He told such a lot of stories,' said Esther Walters, apologetically, 'and as I said, one didn't always listen.'

'He had a snapshot,' said Miss Marple, 'that he used to show people.'

'I believe he did . . . I can't remember what it was now. Did he show it to you?'

'No,' said Miss Marple. 'He didn't show it to me. We were interrupted—'

CHAPTER 9

Miss Prescott and Others

'The story *I* heard,' began Miss Prescott, lowering her voice, and looking carefully around.

Miss Marple drew her chair a little closer. It had been some time before she had been able to get together with Miss Prescott for a heart-to-heart chat. This was owing to the fact that clergymen are very strong family men so that Miss Prescott was nearly always accompanied by her brother, and there was no doubt that Miss Marple and Miss Prescott found it less easy to take their back hair down in a good gossip when the jovial Canon was of their company.

'It seems,' said Miss Prescott, 'though of course I don't want to talk any scandal and I really know *nothing* about it—'

'Oh, I *quite* understand,' said Miss Marple.

'It seems there was some scandal when his first wife was still alive! Apparently this woman, Lucky—such a name!—who I think was a cousin of his first wife, came out here and joined them and I think did some work with

70

him on flowers or butterflies or whatever it was. And people talked a lot because they got on so well together—if you know what I mean.'

'People do *notice* things so much, don't they?' said Miss Marple.

'And then of course, when his wife died rather suddenly—'

'She died here, on this island?'

'No. No, I think they were in Martinique or Tobago at the time.'

'I see.'

'But I gathered from some other people who were there at the time, and who came on here and talked about things, that the doctor wasn't very satisfied.'

'Indeed,' said Miss Marple, with interest.

'It was only *gossip*,' of course, 'but—well, Mr Dyson certainly married again *very quickly*.' She lowered her voice again. 'Only a *month* I believe.'

'Only a month,' said Miss Marple.

The two women looked at each other. 'It seemed—unfeeling,' said Miss Prescott.

'Yes,' said Miss Marple. 'It certainly did.' She added delicately, 'Was there—any money?'

'I don't really know. He makes his little joke—perhaps you've heard him—about his wife being his "lucky piece"—'

'Yes, I've heard him,' said Miss Marple.

'And some people think that means that he was lucky to marry a rich wife. Though, of course,' said Miss Prescott with the air of one being entirely fair, 'she's very good-looking

Agatha Christie

too, if you care for that type. And I think myself that it was the *first* wife who had the money.'

'Are the Hillingdons well off?'

'Well, I think they're *well off*. I don't mean fabulously rich, I just mean well off. They have two boys at public school and a very nice place in England, I believe, and they travel most of the winter.'

The Canon appearing at this moment to suggest a brisk walk, Miss Prescott rose to join her brother. Miss Marple remained sitting there.

A few minutes later Gregory Dyson passed her striding along towards the hotel. He waved a cheerful hand as he passed.

'Penny for your thoughts,' he called out.

Miss Marple smiled gently, wondering how he would have reacted if she had replied:

'I was wondering if you were a murderer.'

It really seemed most probable that he was. It all fitted in so nicely—This story about the death of the first Mrs Dyson—Major Palgrave had certainly been talking about a wife killer—with special reference to the 'Brides in the Bath Case'.

Yes—it fitted—the only objection was that it fitted almost too well. But Miss Marple reproved herself for this thought—who was she to demand Murders Made to Measure?

A voice made her jump—a somewhat raucous one.

'Seen Greg any place, Miss—er—'

Lucky, Miss Marple thought, was not in a good temper.

'He passed by just now—going towards the hotel.'

72

'I'll bet!' Lucky uttered an irritated ejaculation and hurried on.

'Forty, if she's a day, and looks it this morning,' thought Miss Marple.

Pity invaded her—pity for the Luckys of the world—who were so vulnerable to Time—

At the sound of a noise behind her, she turned her chair round—

Mr Rafiel, supported by Jackson, was making his morning appearance and coming out of his bungalow—

Jackson settled his employer in his wheelchair and fussed round him. Mr Rafiel waved his attendant away impatiently and Jackson went off in the direction of the hotel.

Miss Marple lost no time—Mr Rafiel was never left alone for long—Probably Esther Walters would come and join him. Miss Marple wanted a word alone with Mr Rafiel and now, she thought, was her chance. She would have to be quick about what she wanted to say. There could be no leading up to things. Mr Rafiel was not a man who cared for the idle twittering conversation of old ladies. He would probably retreat again into his bungalow, definitely regarding himself the victim of persecution. Miss Marple decided to plump for downrightness.

She made her way to where he was sitting, drew up a chair, sat down, and said:

'I want to ask you something, Mr Rafiel.'

'All right, all right,' said Mr Rafiel, 'let's have it. What do you want—a subscription, I suppose? Missions in Africa or repairing a church, something of that kind?'

'Yes,' said Miss Marple. 'I am interested in several objects of that nature, and I shall be delighted if you will give me a subscription for them. But that wasn't actually what I was going to ask you. What I was going to ask you was if Major Palgrave ever told you a story about a murder.'

'Oho,' said Mr Rafiel. 'So he told it to you too, did he? And I suppose you fell for it, hook, line and sinker.'

'I didn't really know what to think,' said Miss Marple. 'What exactly did he tell you?'

'He prattled on,' said Mr Rafiel, 'about a lovely creature, Lucrezia Borgia reincarnated. Beautiful, young, golden-haired, everything.'

'Oh,' said Miss Marple slightly taken aback, 'and who did she murder?'

'Her husband, of course,' said Mr Rafiel, 'who do you think?'

'Poison?'

'No, I think she gave him a sleeping draught and then stuck him in a gas oven. Resourceful female. Then she said it was suicide. She got off quite lightly. Diminished responsibility or something. That's what it's called nowadays if you're a good-looking woman, or some miserable young hooligan whose mother's been too fond of him. Bah!'

'Did the Major show you a snapshot?'

'What—a snapshot of the woman? No. Why should he?'

'Oh—' said Miss Marple.

She sat there, rather taken aback. Apparently Major Palgrave spent his life telling people not only about tigers

74

he had shot and elephants he had hunted but also about murderers he had met. Perhaps he had a whole repertoire of murder stories. One had to face it—She was startled by Mr Rafiel suddenly giving a roar of 'Jackson!' There was no response.

'Shall I find him for you?' said Miss Marple rising.

'You won't find him. Tom-catting somewhere, that's what he does. No good, that fellow. Bad character. But he suits me all right.'

'I'll go and look for him,' said Miss Marple.

Miss Marple found Jackson sitting on the far side of the hotel terrace having a drink with Tim Kendal.

'Mr Rafiel is asking for you,' she said.

Jackson made an expressive grimace, drained his glass, and rose to his feet.

'Here we go again,' he said. 'No peace for the wicked— Two telephone calls and a special diet order—I thought that might give me a quarter of an hour's alibi—Apparently not! Thank you, Miss Marple. Thanks for the drink, Mr Kendal.'

He strode away.

'I feel sorry for that chap,' said Tim. 'I have to stand him a drink now and then, just to cheer him up—Can I offer you something, Miss Marple—How about fresh lime? I know you're fond of that.'

'Not just now, thank you—I suppose looking after someone like Mr Rafiel must always be rather exacting. Invalids are frequently difficult—'

'I didn't mean only that—It's very well paid and you expect to put up with a good deal of crotchetiness—old

Rafiel's not really a bad sort. I mean more that—' he hesitated.

Miss Marple looked inquiring.

'Well—how shall I put it—it's difficult for him socially. People are so damned snobbish—there's no one here of his class. He's better than a servant—and below the average visitor—or they think he is. Rather like the Victorian governess. Even the secretary woman, Mrs Walters—feels she's a cut above him. Makes things difficult.' Tim paused, then said with feeling: 'It's really awful the amount of social problems there are in a place like this.'

Dr Graham passed them—he had a book in his hand. He went and sat at a table overlooking the sea.

'Dr Graham looks rather worried,' remarked Miss Marple.

'Oh! We're all worried.'

'You too? Because of Major Palgrave's death?'

'I've left off worrying about that. People seem to have forgotten it—taken it in their stride. No—it's my wife—Molly—Do you know anything about dreams?'

'Dreams?' Miss Marple was surprised.

'Yes—bad dreams—nightmares, I suppose. Oh, we all get that sort of thing sometimes. But Molly—she seems to have them nearly all the time. They frighten her. Is there anything one can do about them? Take for them? She's got some sleeping pills, but she says they make it worse—she struggles to wake up and can't.'

'What are the dreams about?'

'Oh, something or someone chasing her—Or watching her and spying on her—she can't shake off the feeling even when she's awake.'

'Surely a doctor—'

'She's got a thing against doctors. Won't hear of it—Oh well—I dare say it will all pass off—But we were so happy. It was all such fun—And now, just lately—Perhaps old Palgrave's death upset her. She seems like a different person since . . .'

He got up.

'Must get on with the daily chores—are you sure you won't have that fresh lime?'

Miss Marple shook her head.

She sat there, thinking. Her face was grave and anxious.

She glanced over at Dr Graham.

Presently she came to a decision.

She rose and went across to his table.

'I have got to apologize to you, Dr Graham,' she said.

'Indeed?' The doctor looked at her in kindly surprise. He pulled forward a chair and she sat down.

'I am afraid I have done the most disgraceful thing,' said Miss Marple. 'I told you, Dr Graham, a deliberate lie.'

She looked at him apprehensively.

Dr Graham did not look at all shattered, but he did look a little surprised.

'Really?' he said. 'Ah well, you mustn't let that worry you too much.'

What had the dear old thing been telling lies about, he wondered; her age? Though as far as he could remember she hadn't mentioned her age. 'Well, let's hear about it,' he said, since she clearly wished to confess.

'You remember my speaking to you about a snapshot of my nephew, one that I showed to Major Palgrave, and that he didn't give back to me?'

'Yes, yes, of course I remember. Sorry we couldn't find it for you.'

'There wasn't any such thing,' said Miss Marple, in a small frightened voice.

'I beg your pardon?'

'There wasn't any such thing. I made up that story, I'm afraid.'

'You made it up?' Dr Graham looked slightly annoyed. 'Why?'

Miss Marple told him. She told him quite clearly, without twittering. She told him about Major Palgrave's murder story and how he'd been about to show her this particular snapshot and his sudden confusion and then she went on to her own anxiety and to her final decision to try somehow to obtain a view of it.

'And really, I couldn't see any way of doing so without telling you something that was quite untrue,' she said, 'I do hope you will forgive me.'

'You thought that what he had been about to show you was a picture of a murderer?'

'That's what he said it was,' said Miss Marple. 'At least he said it was given him by this acquaintance who had told him the story about a man who was a murderer.'

'Yes, yes. And—excuse me—you believed him?'

'I don't know if I really believed him or not at the time,' said Miss Marple. 'But then, you see, the next day he died.'

'Yes,' said Dr Graham, struck suddenly by the clarity of that one sentence. *The next day he died* . . .

'And the snapshot had disappeared.'

Dr Graham looked at her. He didn't know quite what to say.

'Excuse me, Miss Marple,' he said at last, 'but is what you're telling me now—is it really true this time?'

'I don't wonder your doubting me,' said Miss Marple. 'I should, in your place. Yes, it is true what I am telling you now, but I quite realize that you have only my word for it. Still, even if you don't believe me, I thought I ought to tell you.'

'Why?'

'I realized that you ought to have the fullest information possible—in case—'

'In case what?'

'In case you decided to take any steps about it.'

CHAPTER 10

A Decision in Jamestown

Dr Graham was in Jamestown, in the Administrator's office, sitting at a table opposite his friend Daventry, a grave young man of thirty-five.

'You sounded rather mysterious on the phone, Graham,' said Daventry. 'Anything special the matter?'

'I don't know,' said Dr Graham, 'but I'm worried.'

Daventry looked at the other's face, then he nodded as drinks were brought in. He spoke lightly of a fishing expedition he had made lately. Then when the servant had gone away, he sat back in his chair and looked at the other man.

'Now then,' he said, 'let's have it.'

Dr Graham recounted the facts that had worried him. Daventry gave a slow long whistle.

'I see. You think maybe there's something funny about old Palgrave's death? You're no longer sure that it was just natural causes? Who certified the death? Robertson, I suppose. He didn't have any doubts, did he?'

'No, but I think he may have been influenced in giving

80

the certificate by the fact of the Serenite tablets in the bathroom. He asked me if Palgrave had mentioned that he suffered from hypertension, and I said No, I'd never had any medical conversation with him myself, but apparently he had talked about it to other people in the hotel. The whole thing—the bottle of tablets, and what Palgrave had said to people—it all fitted in—no earthly reason to suspect anything else. It was a perfectly natural inference to make—but I think now it may not have been correct. If it had been my business to give the certificate, I'd have given it without a second thought. The appearances are quite consistent with his having died from that cause. I'd never have thought about it since if it hadn't been for the odd disappearance of that snapshot . . .'

'But look here, Graham,' said Daventry, 'if you will allow me to say so, aren't you relying a little too much on a rather fanciful story told you by an elderly lady? You know what these elderly ladies are like. They magnify some small detail and work the whole thing up.'

'Yes, I know,' said Dr Graham, unhappily. 'I know that. I've said to myself that it may be so, that it probably *is* so. But I can't quite convince myself. She was so very clear and detailed in her statement.'

'The whole thing seems wildly improbable to me,' said Daventry. 'Some old lady tells a story about a snapshot that ought not to be there—no, I'm getting mixed myself— I mean the other way about, don't I?—but the only thing you've really got to go on is that a chambermaid says that a bottle of pills which the authorities had relied on for evidence, wasn't in the Major's room the day before his death. But there are a hundred explanations for that. He might always have carried those pills about in his pocket.'

'It's possible, I suppose, yes.'

'Or the chambermaid may have made a mistake and she simply hadn't noticed them before—'

'That's possible, too.'

'Well, then.'

Graham said slowly:

'The girl was very positive.'

'Well, the St Honoré people are very excitable. You know. Emotional. Work themselves up easily. Are you thinking that she knows—a little more than she has said?'

'I think it might be so,' said Dr Graham slowly.

'You'd better try and get it out of her, if so. We don't want to make an unnecessary fuss—unless we've something definite to go on. If he didn't die of blood pressure, what do you think it was?'

'There are too many things it might be nowadays,' said Dr Graham.

'You mean things that don't leave recognizable traces?'

'Not everyone,' said Dr Graham dryly, 'is so considerate as to use arsenic.'

'Now let's get things quite clear—what's the suggestion? That a bottle of pills was substituted for the real ones? And that Major Palgrave was poisoned in that way?'

'No—it's not like that. That's what the girl—Victoria Something thinks—But she's got it all wrong—If it was decided to get rid of the Major—quickly—he would have been given something—most likely in a drink of some kind. Then to make it appear a natural death, a bottle of the tablets prescribed to relieve blood pressure was put in his room. And the rumour was put about that he suffered from high blood pressure.'

'Who put the rumour about?'

'I've tried to find out—with no success—It's been too cleverly done. A says "I *think* B told me"—B, asked, says "No, I didn't say so but I do remember C mentioning it one day." C says "Several people talked about it—one of them, I think, was A." And there we are, back again.'

'Someone was clever?'

'Yes. As soon as the death was discovered, everybody seemed to be talking about the Major's high blood pressure and repeating round what other people had said.'

'Wouldn't it have been simpler just to poison him and let it go at that?'

'No. That might have meant an inquiry—possibly an autopsy—This way, a doctor would accept the death and give a certificate—as he did.'

'What do you want me to do? Go to the CID? Suggest they dig the chap up? It'd make a lot of stink—'

'It could be kept quite quiet.'

'Could it? In St Honoré? Think again! The grapevine would be on to it before it had happened. All the same,' Daventry sighed—'I suppose we'll have to do something. But if you ask me, it's all a mare's nest!'

'I devoutly hope it is,' said Dr Graham.

CHAPTER 11

Evening at the Golden Palm

Molly rearranged a few of the table decorations in the dining-room, removed an extra knife, straightened a fork, reset a glass or two, stood back to look at the effect and then walked out on to the terrace outside. There was no one about just at present and she strolled to the far corner and stood by the balustrade. Soon another evening would begin. Chattering, talking, drinking, all so gay and care-free, the sort of life she had longed for and, up to a few days ago, had enjoyed so much. Now even Tim seemed anxious and worried. Natural, perhaps, that he should worry a little. It was important that this venture of theirs should turn out all right. After all, he had sunk all he had in it.

But that, thought Molly, is not *really* what's worrying him. It's *me*. But I don't see, said Molly to herself, why he should worry about *me*. Because he did worry about her. That she was quite sure of. The questions he put, the quick nervous glance he shot at her from time to time. 'But why?' thought Molly. 'I've been very careful.'

She summed up things in her mind. She didn't understand it really herself. She couldn't remember when it had begun. She wasn't even very sure what it was. She'd begun to be frightened of people. She didn't know why. What could they do to her? What should they want to do to her?

She nodded her head, then started violently as a hand touched her arm. She spun round to find Gregory Dyson, slightly taken aback, looking apologetic.

'Ever so sorry. Did I startle you, little girl?'

Molly hated being called 'little girl'. She said quickly and brightly: 'I didn't hear you coming, Mr Dyson, so it made me jump.'

'Mr Dyson? We're very formal tonight. Aren't we all one great happy family here? Ed and me and Lucky and Evelyn and you and Tim and Esther Walters and old Rafiel. All the lot of us one happy family.'

'He's had plenty to drink already,' thought Molly. She smiled at him pleasantly.

'Oh! I come over the heavy hostess sometimes,' she said, lightly. 'Tim and I think it's more polite not to be too handy with Christian names.'

'Aw! we don't want any of that stuffed-shirt business. Now then, Molly my lovely, have a drink with me.'

'Ask me later,' said Molly. 'I have a few things to get on with.'

'Now don't run away.' His arm fastened round her arm. 'You're a lovely girl, Molly. I hope Tim appreciates his good luck.'

'Oh, I see to it that he does,' said Molly cheerfully.

'I could go for you, you know, in a big way.' He leered at her—'though I wouldn't let my wife hear me say so.'

'Did you have a good trip this afternoon?'

'I suppose so. Between you and me I get a bit fed up sometimes. You can get tired of the birds and butterflies. What say you and I go for a little picnic on our own one day?'

'We'll have to see about that,' said Molly gaily. 'I'll be looking forward to it.'

With a light laugh she escaped, and went back into the bar.

'Hallo, Molly,' said Tim, 'you seem in a hurry. Who's that you've been with out there?'

He peered out.

'Gregory Dyson.'

'What does he want?'

'Wanted to make a pass at me,' said Molly.

'Blast him,' said Tim.

'Don't worry,' said Molly, 'I can do all the blasting necessary.'

Tim started to answer her, caught sight of Fernando and went over to him shouting out some directions. Molly slipped away through the kitchen door and down the steps to the beach.

Gregory Dyson swore under his breath. Then he walked slowly back in the direction of his bungalow. He had nearly got there when a voice spoke to him from the shadow of one of the bushes. He turned his head, startled. In the gathering dusk he thought for a moment that it was a ghostly figure that stood there. Then he laughed. It had looked like a faceless apparition but that was because, though the dress was white, the face was black.

Victoria stepped out of the bushes on to the path.

'Mr Dyson, please?'

'Yes. What is it?'

Ashamed of being startled, he spoke with a touch of impatience.

'I brought you this, sir.' She held out her hand. In it was a bottle of tablets. 'This belongs to you, doesn't it? Yes?'

'Oh, my bottle of Serenite tablets. Yes, of course. Where did you find it?'

'I found it where it had been put. In the gentleman's room.'

'What do you mean—in the gentleman's room?'

'The gentleman who is dead,' she added gravely. 'I do not think he sleeps very well in his grave.'

'Why the devil not?' asked Dyson.

Victoria stood looking at him.

'I still don't know what you're talking about. You mean you found this bottle of tablets in Major Palgrave's bungalow?'

'That's right, yes. After the doctor and the Jamestown people go away, they give me all the things in his bathroom to throw away. The toothpaste and the lotions, and all the other things—including this.'

'Well, why didn't you throw it away?'

'Because these are yours. You missed them. You remember, you asked about them?'

'Yes—well—yes, I did. I—I thought I'd just mislaid them.'

'No, you did not mislay them. They were taken from your bungalow and put in Major Palgrave's bungalow.'

'How do you know?' He spoke roughly.

'I know. I saw.' She smiled at him in a sudden flash of white teeth. 'Someone put them in the dead gentleman's room. Now I give them back to you.'

'Here—wait. What do you mean? What—who did you see?'

She hurried away, back into the darkness of the bushes. Greg made as to move after her and then stopped. He stood stroking his chin.

'What's the matter, Greg? Seen a ghost?' asked Mrs Dyson, as she came along the path from their bungalow.

'Thought I had for a minute or two.'

'Who was that you were talking to?'

'The coloured girl who does our place. Victoria, her name is, isn't it?'

'What did she want? Making a pass at you?'

'Don't be stupid, Lucky. That girl's got some idiotic idea into her head.'

'Idea about what?'

'You remember I couldn't find my Serenite the other day?'

'You said you couldn't.'

'What do you mean "I said I couldn't"?'

'Oh, for heck's sake, have you got to take me up on everything?'

'I'm sorry,' said Greg. 'Everybody goes about being so

damn' mysterious.' He held out his hand with the bottle in it. 'That girl brought them back to me.'

'Had she pinched them?'

'No. She—found them somewhere I think.'

'Well, what of it? What's the mystery about?'

'Oh, nothing,' said Greg. 'She just riled me, that's all.'

'Look here, Greg, what is this stuff all about? Come along and have a drink before dinner.'

Molly had gone down to the beach. She pulled out one of the old basket chairs, one of the more rickety ones that were seldom used. She sat in it for a while looking at the sea, then suddenly she dropped her head in her hands and burst into tears. She sat there sobbing unrestrainedly for some time. Then she heard a rustle close by her and glanced up sharply to see Mrs Hillingdon looking down at her.

'Hallo, Evelyn, I didn't hear you. I—I'm sorry.'

'What's the matter, child?' said Evelyn. 'Something gone wrong?' She pulled another chair forward and sat down. 'Tell me.'

'There's nothing wrong,' said Molly. 'Nothing at all.'

'Of course there is. You wouldn't sit and cry here for nothing. Can't you tell me? Is it—some trouble between you and Tim?'

'Oh *no*.'

'I'm glad of that. You always look so happy together.'

'Not more than you do,' said Molly. 'Tim and I always think how wonderful it is that you and Edward should seem so happy together after being married so many years.'

'Oh, that,' said Evelyn. Her voice was sharp as she spoke but Molly hardly noticed.

'People bicker so,' she said, 'and have such rows. Even if they're quite fond of each other they still seem to have rows and not to mind a bit whether they have them in public or not.'

'Some people like living that way,' said Evelyn. 'It doesn't really mean anything.'

'Well, I think it's horrid,' said Molly.

'So do I, really,' said Evelyn.

'But to see you and Edward—'

'Oh it's no good, Molly. I can't let you go on thinking things of that kind. Edward and I—' she paused. 'If you want to know the truth, we've hardly said a word to each other in private for the last three years.'

'What!' Molly stared at her, appalled. 'I—I can't believe it.'

'Oh, we both put up quite a good show,' said Evelyn. 'We're neither of us the kind that like having rows in public. And anyway there's nothing really to have a row about.'

'But what went wrong?' asked Molly.

'Just the usual.'

'What do you mean by the usual? Another—'

'Yes, another woman in the case, and I don't suppose it will be difficult for you to guess who the woman is.'

'Do you mean Mrs Dyson—Lucky?'

Evelyn nodded.

'I know they always flirt together a lot,' said Molly, 'but I thought that was just . . .'

'Just high spirits?' said Evelyn. 'Nothing behind it?'

'But why—' Molly paused and tried again. 'But didn't you—oh I mean, well I suppose I oughtn't to ask.'

'Ask anything you like,' said Evelyn. 'I'm tired of never saying a word, tired of being a well-bred happy wife. Edward just lost his head completely about Lucky. He was stupid enough to come and tell me about it. It made him feel better I suppose. Truthful. Honourable. All that sort of stuff. It didn't occur to him to think that it wouldn't make *me* feel better.'

'Did he want to leave you?'

Evelyn shook her head. 'We've got two children, you know,' she said. 'Children whom we're both very fond of. They're at school in England. We didn't want to break up the home. And then of course, Lucky didn't want a divorce either. Greg's a very rich man. His first wife left a lot of money. So we agreed to live and let live—Edward and Lucky in happy immorality, Greg in blissful ignorance, and Edward and I just good friends.' She spoke with scalding bitterness.

'How—how can you bear it?'

'One gets used to anything. But sometimes—'

'Yes?' said Molly.

'Sometimes I'd like to kill that woman.'

The passion behind her voice startled Molly.

'Don't let's talk any more about me,' said Evelyn. 'Let's talk about you. I want to know what's the matter.'

Molly was silent for some moments and then she said, 'It's only—it's only that I think there's something wrong about me.'

'Wrong? What do you mean?'

Molly shook her head unhappily. 'I'm frightened,' she said. 'I'm terribly frightened.'

'Frightened of what?'

'Everything,' said Molly. 'It's—growing on me. Voices in the bushes, footsteps—or things that people say. As though someone were watching me all the time, spying on me. Somebody hates me. That's what I keep feeling. Somebody hates me.'

'My dear child.' Evelyn was shocked and startled. 'How long has this been going on?'

'I don't know. It came—it started by degrees. And there have been other things too.'

'What sort of things?'

'There are times,' said Molly slowly, 'that I can't account for, that I can't remember.'

'Do you mean you have blackouts—that sort of thing?'

'I suppose so. I mean sometimes it's—oh, say it's five o'clock—and I can't remember anything since about half past one or two.'

'Oh my dear, but that's just that you've been asleep. Had a doze.'

'No,' said Molly, 'it's not like that at all. Because you see, at the end of the time it's not as though I'd just dozed off. I'm in a different *place*. Sometimes I'm wearing different clothes and sometimes I seem to have been doing things—even saying things to people, talked to someone, and not remembering that I've done so.'

Evelyn looked shocked. 'But Molly, my dear, if this is so, then you ought to see a doctor.'

'I won't see a doctor! I don't want to. I wouldn't go *near* a doctor.'

Evelyn looked sharply down into her face, then she took the girl's hand in hers.

'You may be frightening yourself for nothing, Molly. You know there are all kinds of nervous disorders that aren't really serious at all. A doctor would soon reassure you.'

'He mightn't. He might say that there was something really wrong with me.'

'Why should there be anything wrong with you?'

'Because—' Molly spoke and then was silent, '—no reason, I suppose,' she said.

'Couldn't your family—haven't you any family, any mother or sisters or someone who could come out here?'

'I don't get on with my mother. I never have. I've got sisters. They're married but I suppose—I suppose they could come if I wanted them. But I don't want them. I don't want anyone—anyone except Tim.'

'Does Tim know about this? Have you told him?'

'Not really,' said Molly. 'But he's anxious about me and he watches me. It's as though he were trying to—to help me or to shield me. But if he does that it means I want shielding, doesn't it?'

'I think a lot of it may be imagination but I still think you ought to see a doctor.'

'Old Dr Graham? He wouldn't be any good.'

'There are other doctors on the island.'

'It's all right, really,' said Molly. 'I just—mustn't think of it. I expect, as you say, it's all imagination. Good

93

Agatha Christie

gracious, it's getting frightfully late. I ought to be on duty now in the dining-room. I—I must go back.'

She looked sharply and almost offensively at Evelyn Hillingdon, and then hurried off. Evelyn stared after her.

CHAPTER 12

Old Sins Cast Long Shadows

'I think as I am on to something, man.'

'What's that you say, Victoria?'

'I think I'm on to something. It may mean money. Big money.'

'Now look, girl, you be careful, you'll not tangle yourself up in something. Maybe I'd better tackle what it is.'

Victoria laughed, a deep rich chuckle.

'You wait and see,' she said. 'I know how to play this hand. It's money, man, it's big money. Something I see, and something I guess. I think I guess right.'

And again the soft rich chuckle rolled out on the night.

'Evelyn . . .'

'Yes?'

Evelyn Hillingdon spoke mechanically, without interest. She did not look at her husband.

'Evelyn, would you mind if we chucked all this and went home to England?'

95

She had been combing her short dark hair. Now her hands came down from her head sharply. She turned towards him.

'You mean—but we've only just come. We've not been out here in the islands for more than three weeks.'

'I know. But—would you mind?'

Her eyes searched him incredulously.

'You really want to go back to England? Back home?'

'Yes.'

'Leaving—Lucky?'

He winced.

'You've known all the time, I suppose, that—that it was going on?'

'Pretty well. Yes.'

'You've never said anything.'

'Why should I? We had the whole thing out years ago. Neither of us wanted to make a break. So we agreed to go our separate ways—but keep up the show in public.' Then she added before he could speak, 'But why are you so set on going back to England *now*?'

'Because I'm at breaking point. I can't stick it any longer, Evelyn. I can't.' The quiet Edward Hillingdon was transformed. His hands shook, he swallowed, his calm unemotional face seemed distorted by pain.

'For God's sake, Edward, what's the *matter*?'

'Nothing's the matter except that I want to get out of here—'

'You fell wildly in love with Lucky. And now you've got over it. Is that what you're telling me?'

'Yes. I don't suppose you'll ever feel the same.'

'Oh let's not go into that now! I want to understand what's upsetting you so much, Edward.'

'I'm not particularly upset.'

'But you are. Why?'

'Isn't it obvious?'

'No, it isn't,' said Evelyn. 'Let's put it in plain concrete terms. You've had an affair with a woman. That happens often enough. And now it's over. Or isn't it over? Perhaps it isn't over on *her* side. Is that it? Does Greg know about it? I've often wondered.'

'I don't know,' said Edward. 'He's never said anything. He always seems friendly enough.'

'Men can be extraordinarily obtuse,' said Evelyn thoughtfully. 'Or else—Perhaps Greg has got an outside interest of his own!'

'He's made passes at you, hasn't he?' said Edward. 'Answer me—I know he has—'

'Oh yes,' said Evelyn, carelessly, 'but he makes passes at everyone. That's just Greg. It doesn't ever really mean much, I imagine. It's just part of the Greg he-man act.'

'Do you care for him, Evelyn? I'd rather know the truth.'

'Greg? I'm quite fond of him—he amuses me. He's a good friend.'

'And that's all? I wish I could believe you.'

'I can't really see how it can possibly matter to you,' said Evelyn dryly.

'I suppose I deserve that.'

Evelyn walked to the window, looked out across the veranda and came back again.

'I wish you would tell me what's *really* upsetting you, Edward.'

'I've told you.'

'I wonder.'

'You can't understand, I suppose, how extraordinary a temporary madness of this kind can seem to you after you've got over it.'

'I can try, I suppose. But what's worrying me now is that Lucky seems to have got some kind of stranglehold upon you. She's not just a discarded mistress. She's a tigress with claws. You *must* tell me the truth, Edward. It's the only way if you want me to stand by you.'

Edward said in a low voice: 'If I don't get away from her soon—I shall kill her.'

'Kill Lucky? Why?'

'Because of what she made me do . . .'

'What did she make you do?'

'I helped her to commit a murder—'

The words were out—There was silence—Evelyn stared at him.

'Do you know what you are saying?'

'Yes. I didn't know I was doing it. There were things she asked me to get for her—at the chemist's. I didn't know—I hadn't the least idea what she wanted them for—She got me to copy out a prescription she had . . .'

'When was this?'

'Four years ago. When we were in Martinique. When—when Greg's wife—'

'You mean Greg's first wife—Gail? You mean Lucky poisoned her?'

'Yes—and I helped her. When I realized—'

Evelyn interrupted him.

'When you realized what had happened, Lucky pointed out to you that *you* had written out the prescription, that *you* had got the drugs, that you and she were in it together? Is that right?'

'Yes. She said she had done it out of pity—that Gail was suffering—that she had begged Lucky to get something that would end it all.'

'A mercy killing! I see. And you believed *that*?'

Edward Hillingdon was silent a moment—then he said:

'No—I didn't really—not deep down—I accepted it because I *wanted* to believe it—because I was infatuated with Lucky.'

'And afterwards—when she married Greg—did you still believe it?'

'I'd made myself believe it by then.'

'And Greg—how much did he know about it all?'

'Nothing at all.'

'That I find hard to believe!'

Edward Hillingdon broke out—

'Evelyn, I've *got* to get free of it all! That woman taunts me still with what I did. She knows I don't care for her any longer. Care for her?—I've come to hate her—But she makes me feel I'm tied to her—by the thing we did together—'

Evelyn walked up and down the room—then she stopped and faced him.

'The entire trouble with you, Edward, is that you are ridiculously sensitive—and also incredibly suggestible.

Agatha Christie

That devil of a woman has got you just where she wants you by playing on your sense of guilt—And I'll tell you this in plain Bible terms, the guilt that weighs on you is the guilt of adultery—not murder—you were guilt-stricken about your affair with Lucky—and then she made a cat's-paw of you for her murder scheme, and managed to make you feel you shared her guilt. You *don't*.'

'Evelyn . . .' He stepped towards her—

She stepped back a minute—and looked at him searchingly.

'Is this all true, Edward—*Is* it? Or are you making it up?'

'Evelyn! Why on earth should I do such a thing?'

'I don't know,' said Evelyn Hillingdon slowly—'It's just perhaps—because I find it hard to trust—anybody. And because—Oh! I don't know—I've got, I suppose, so that I don't know the truth when I hear it.'

'Let's chuck all this—Go back home to England.'

'Yes—We will—But not now.'

'Why not?'

'We must carry on as usual—just for the present. It's important. Do you understand, Edward? Don't let Lucky have an inkling of what we're up to—'

CHAPTER 13

Exit Victoria Johnson

The evening was drawing to a close. The steel band was at last relaxing its efforts. Tim stood by the dining-room looking over the terrace. He extinguished a few lights on tables that had been vacated.

A voice spoke behind him. 'Tim, can I speak to you a moment?'

Tim Kendal started.

'Hallo, Evelyn, is there anything I can do for you?'

Evelyn looked round.

'Come to this table here, and let's sit down a minute.'

She led the way to a table at the extreme end of the terrace. There were no other people near them.

'Tim, you must forgive me talking to you, but I'm worried about Molly.'

His face changed at once.

'What about Molly?' he said stiffly.

'I don't think she's awfully well. She seems upset.'

'Things do seem to upset her rather easily just lately.'

'She ought to see a doctor, I think.'

101

'Yes, I know, but she doesn't want to. She'd hate it.'

'Why?'

'Eh? What d'you mean?'

'I said why? Why should she hate seeing a doctor?'

'Well,' said Tim rather vaguely, 'people do sometimes, you know. It's—well, it sort of makes them feel frightened about themselves.'

'You're worried about her yourself, aren't you, Tim?'

'Yes. Yes, I am rather.'

'Isn't there anyone of her family who could come out here to be with her?'

'No. That'd make things worse, far worse.'

'What *is* the trouble—with her family, I mean?'

'Oh, just one of those things. I suppose she's just highly strung and—she didn't get on with them—particularly her mother. She never has. They're—they're rather an odd family in some ways and she cut loose from them. Good thing she did, I think.'

Evelyn said hesitantly—'She seems to have had blackouts, from what she told me, and to be frightened of people. Almost like persecution mania.'

'Don't say that,' said Tim angrily. 'Persecution mania! People always say that about people. Just because she—well—maybe she's a bit nervy. Coming out here to the West Indies. All the dark faces. You know, people are rather queer, sometimes, about the West Indies and coloured people.'

'Surely not girls like Molly?'

'Oh, how does one know the things people are frightened of? There are people who can't be in the room with

102

cats. And other people who faint if a caterpillar drops on them.'

'I hate suggesting it—but don't you think perhaps she ought to see a—well, a psychiatrist?'

'*No!*' said Tim explosively. 'I won't have people like that monkeying about with her. I don't believe in them. They make people worse. If her mother had left psychiatrists alone . . .'

'So there *was* trouble of that kind in her family—was there? I mean a history of—' she chose the word carefully—'instability.'

'I don't want to talk about it—I took her away from it all and she was all right, quite all right. She has just got into a nervous state . . . But these things aren't hereditary. Everybody knows that nowadays. It's an exploded idea. Molly's perfectly sane. It's just that—oh! I believe it was that wretched old Palgrave dying that started it all off.'

'I see,' said Evelyn thoughtfully. 'But there was nothing really to worry anyone in Major Palgrave's death, was there?'

'No, of course there wasn't. But it's a kind of shock when somebody dies suddenly.'

He looked so desperate and defeated that Evelyn's heart smote her. She put her hand on his arm.

'Well, I hope you know what you're doing, Tim, but if I could help in any way—I mean if I could go with Molly to New York—I could fly with her there or Miami or somewhere where she could get really first-class medical advice.'

'It's very good of you, Evelyn, but Molly's all right. She's getting over it, anyway.'

Evelyn shook her head in doubt. She turned away slowly and looked along the line of the terrace. Most people had gone by now to their bungalows. Evelyn was walking towards her table to see if she'd left anything behind there, when she heard Tim give an exclamation. She looked up sharply. He was staring towards the steps at the end of the terrace and she followed his gaze. Then she too caught her breath.

Molly was coming up the steps from the beach. She was breathless with deep, sobbing breaths, her body swayed to and fro as she came, in a curious directionless run. Tim cried:

'*Molly!* What's the matter?'

He ran towards her and Evelyn followed him. Molly was at the top of the steps now and she stood there, both hands behind her back. She said in sobbing breaths:

'I found her . . . She's there in the bushes . . . There in the bushes . . . And look at my hands—look at my *hands*.' She held them out and Evelyn caught her breath as she saw the queer dark stains. They looked dark in the subdued lighting but she knew well enough that their real colour was red.

'What's happened, Molly?' cried Tim.

'Down there,' said Molly. She swayed on her feet. 'In the bushes . . .'

Tim hesitated, looked at Evelyn, then shoved Molly a little towards Evelyn and ran down the steps. Evelyn put her arm round the girl.

'Come. Sit down, Molly. Here. You'd better have something to drink.'

Molly collapsed in a chair and leaned forward on the table, her forehead on her crossed arm. Evelyn did not question her any more. She thought it better to leave her time to recover.

'It'll be all right, you know,' said Evelyn gently. 'It'll be all right.'

'I don't know,' said Molly. 'I don't know what happened. I don't know anything. I can't remember. I—' she raised her head suddenly. 'What's the matter with me? What's the *matter* with me?'

'It's all right, child. It's all right.'

Tim was coming slowly up the steps. His face was ghastly. Evelyn looked up at him, raising her eyebrows in a query.

'It's one of our girls,' he said. 'What's-her-name— Victoria. Somebody's put a knife in her.'

CHAPTER 14

Inquiry

Molly lay on her bed. Dr Graham and Dr Robertson, the West Indian police doctor, stood on one side—Tim on the other. Robertson had his hand on Molly's pulse—He nodded to the man at the foot of the bed, a slender dark man in police uniform, Inspector Weston of the St Honoré Police Force.

'A bare statement—no more,' the doctor said.

The other nodded.

'Now, Mrs Kendal—just tell us how you came to find this girl.'

For a moment or two it was as though the figure on the bed had not heard. Then she spoke in a faint, faraway voice.

'In the bushes—white . . .'

'You saw something white—and you looked to see what it was? Is that it?'

'Yes—white—lying there—I tried—tried to lift—she it—blood—blood all over my hands.'

She began to tremble.

Dr Graham shook his head at them. Robertson whispered—'She can't stand much more.'

'What were you doing on the beach path, Mrs Kendal?'

'Warm—nice—by the sea—'

'You knew who the girl was?'

'Victoria—nice—nice girl—laughs—she used to laugh—oh! and now she won't—She won't ever laugh again. I'll never forget it—I'll never forget it—' Her voice rose hysterically.

'Molly—don't.' It was Tim.

'Quiet—Quiet—' Dr Robertson spoke with a soothing authority—'Just relax—relax—Now just a small prick—' He withdrew the hypodermic.

'She'll be in no fit condition to be questioned for at least twenty-four hours,' he said—'I'll let you know when.'

The big handsome negro looked from one to the other of the men sitting at the table.

'Ah declare to God,' he said. 'That's all Ah know. Ah don't know nothing but what Ah've told you.'

The perspiration stood out on his forehead. Daventry sighed. The man presiding at the table, Inspector Weston of the St Honoré CID, made a gesture of dismissal. Big Jim Ellis shuffled out of the room.

'It's not all he knows, of course,' Weston said. He had the soft Island voice. 'But it's all we shall learn from him.'

'You think he's in the clear himself?' asked Daventry.

'Yes. They seem to have been on good terms together.'

'They weren't married?'

A faint smile appeared on Lieutenant Weston's lips. 'No,' he said, 'they weren't married. We don't have so many marriages on the Island. They christen the children, though. He's had two children by Victoria.'

'Do you think he was in it, whatever it was, with her?'

'Probably not. I think he'd have been nervous of anything of that kind. And I'd say, too, that what she did know wasn't very much.'

'But enough for blackmail?'

'I don't know that I'd even call it that. I doubt if the girl would even understand that word. Payment for being discreet isn't thought of as blackmail. You see, some of the people who stay here are the rich playboy lot and their morals won't bear much investigation.' His voice was slightly scathing.

'We get all kinds, I agree,' said Daventry. 'A woman, maybe, doesn't want it known that she's sleeping around, so she gives a present to the girl who waits on her. It's tacitly understood that the payment's for discretion.'

'Exactly.'

'But this,' objected Daventry, 'wasn't anything of *that* kind. It was murder.'

'I should doubt, though, if the girl knew it was serious. She saw something, some puzzling incident, something to do presumably with this bottle of pills. It belonged to Mr Dyson, I understand. We'd better see him next.'

Gregory came in with his usual hearty air.

'Here I am,' he said, 'what can I do to help? Too bad about this girl. She was a nice girl. We both liked her. I suppose it was some sort of quarrel or other with a man, but she seemed quite happy and no signs of being in trouble about anything. I was kidding her only last night.'

'I believe you take a preparation, Mr Dyson, called Serenite?'

'Quite right. Little pink tablets.'

'You have them on prescription from a physician?'

'Yes. I can show it to you if you like. Suffer a bit from high blood pressure, like so many people do nowadays.'

'Very few people seem to be aware of that fact.'

'Well, I don't go talking about it. I—well, I've always been well and hearty and I never like people who talk about their ailments all the time.'

'How many of the pills do you take?'

'Two, three times a day.'

'Do you have a fairly large stock with you?'

'Yes. I've got about half a dozen bottles. But they're locked up, you know, in a suitcase. I only keep out one, the one that's in current use.'

'And you missed this bottle a short time ago, so I hear?'

'Quite right.'

'And you asked this girl, Victoria Johnson, whether she'd seen it?'

'Yes, I did.'

'And what did she say?'

'She said the last time she'd seen it was on the shelf in our bathroom. She said she'd looked around.'

'And after that?'

'She came and returned the bottle to me some time later. She said was this the bottle that was missing?'

'And you said?'

'I said, "That's it, all right, where did you find it?" and she said it was in old Major Palgrave's room. I said, "How on earth did it get there?"'

'And what did she answer to that?'

'She said she didn't know, but—' he hesitated.

'Yes, Mr Dyson?'

'Well, she gave me the feeling that she did know a little more than she was saying, but I didn't pay much attention. After all, it wasn't very important. As I say, I've got other bottles of the pills with me. I thought perhaps I'd left it around in the restaurant or somewhere and old Palgrave picked it up for some reason. Perhaps he put it in his pocket meaning to return it to me, then forgot.'

'And that's all you know about it, Mr Dyson?'

'That's all I know. Sorry to be so unhelpful. Is it important? Why?'

Weston shrugged his shoulders. 'As things are, anything may be important.'

'I don't see where pills come in. I thought you'd want to know about what my movements were when this wretched girl was stabbed. I've written them all down as carefully as I can.'

Weston looked at him thoughtfully.

'Indeed? That was very helpful of you, Mr Dyson.'

'Save everybody trouble, I thought,' said Greg. He shoved a piece of paper across the table.

Weston studied it and Daventry drew his chair a little closer and looked over his shoulder.

'That seems very clear,' said Weston, after a moment or two. 'You and your wife were together changing for

110

dinner in your bungalow until ten minutes to nine. You then went along to the terrace where you had drinks with Señora de Caspearo. At quarter past nine Colonel and Mrs Hillingdon joined you and you went in to dine. As far as you can remember, you went off to bed at about half past eleven.'

'Of course,' said Greg, 'I don't know what time the girl was actually killed—?'

There was a faint semblance of a question in the words. Lieutenant Weston, however, did not appear to notice it.

'Mrs Kendal found her, I understand? Must have been a very nasty shock for her.'

'Yes. Dr Robertson had to give her a sedative.'

'This was quite late, wasn't it, when most people had trundled off to bed?'

'Yes.'

'Had she been dead long? When Mrs Kendal found her, I mean?'

'We're not quite certain of the exact time yet,' said Weston smoothly.

'Poor little Molly. It must have been a nasty shock for her. Matter of fact, I didn't notice *her* about last night. Thought she might have had a headache or something and was lying down.'

'When was the last time you *did* see Mrs Kendal?'

'Oh, quite early, before I went to change. She was playing about with some of the table decorations and things. Rearranging the knives.'

'I see.'

'She was quite cheerful then,' said Greg. 'Kidding and

111

all that. She's a great girl. We're all very fond of her. Tim's a lucky fellow.'

'Well, thank you, Mr Dyson. You can't remember anything more than you've told us about what the girl Victoria said when she returned the tablets?'

'No . . . It was just as I say. Asked me were these the tablets I'd been asking for. Said she'd found them in old Palgrave's room.'

'She'd no idea who put them there?'

'Don't think so—can't remember, really.'

'Thank you, Mr Dyson.'

Gregory went out.

'Very thoughtful of him,' said Weston, gently tapping the paper with his fingernail, 'to be so anxious to want us to know for sure exactly where he was last night.'

'A little over-anxious, do you think?' asked Daventry.

'That's very difficult to tell. There are people, you know, who are naturally nervous about their own safety, about being mixed up with anything. It isn't necessarily because they have any guilty knowledge. On the other hand it might be just that.'

'What about opportunity? Nobody's really got much of an alibi, what with the band and the dancing and the coming and going. People are getting up, leaving their tables, coming back. Women go to powder their noses. Men take a stroll. Dyson could have slipped away. Anybody could have slipped away. But he does seem rather anxious to prove that *he* didn't.' He looked thoughtfully down at the paper. 'So Mrs Kendal was rearranging knives on the table,' he said. 'I rather wonder if he dragged that in on purpose.'

'Did it sound like it to you?'

The other considered. 'I think it's possible.'

Outside the room where the two men were sitting, a noise had arisen. A high voice was demanding admittance shrilly.

'I've got something to tell. I've got something to tell. You take me in to where the gentlemen are. You take me in to where the policeman is.'

A uniformed policeman pushed open the door.

'It's one of the cooks here,' he said, 'very anxious to see you. Says he's got something you ought to know.'

A frightened dark man in a cook's cap pushed past him and came into the room. It was one of the minor cooks. A Cuban, not a native of St Honoré.

'I tell you something. I tell you,' he said. 'She come through my kitchen, she did, and she had a knife with her. A knife, I tell you. She had a knife in her hand. She come through my kitchen and out the door. Out into the garden. I saw her.'

'Now calm down,' said Daventry, 'calm down. Who are you talking about?'

'I tell you who I'm talking about. I'm talking about the boss's wife. Mrs Kendal. I'm talking about her. She have a knife in her hand and she go out into the dark. Before dinner that was—and *she didn't come back*.'

CHAPTER 15

Inquiry Continued

'Can we have a word with you, Mr Kendal?'

'Of course.' Tim looked up from his desk. He pushed some papers aside and indicated chairs. His face was drawn and miserable. 'How are you getting on? Got any forwarder? There seems to be a doom in this place. People are wanting to leave, you know, asking about air passages. Just when it seemed everything was being a success. Oh Lord, you don't know what it means, this place, to me and to Molly. We staked everything on it.'

'It's very hard on you, I know,' said Inspector Weston. 'Don't think that we don't sympathize.'

'If it all could be cleared up quickly,' said Tim. 'This wretched girl Victoria—Oh! I oughtn't to talk about her like that. She was quite a good sort, Victoria was. But— but there must be some quite simple reason, some—kind of intrigue, or love affair she had. Perhaps her husband—'

'Jim Ellis wasn't her husband, and they seemed a settled sort of couple.'

'If it could only be cleared up *quickly*,' said Tim again.

'I'm sorry. You wanted to talk to me about something, ask me something.'

'Yes. It was about last night. According to medical evidence Victoria was killed some time between 10.30 pm and midnight. Alibis under the circumstances that prevail here are not very easy to prove. People are moving about, dancing, walking away from the terrace, coming back. It's all very difficult.'

'I suppose so. But does that mean that you definitely consider Victoria was killed by one of the guests here?'

'Well, we have to examine that possibility, Mr Kendal. What I want to ask you particularly about, is a statement made by one of your cooks.'

'Oh? Which one? What does he say?'

'He's a Cuban, I understand.'

'We've got two Cubans and a Puerto Rican.'

'This man Enrico states that your wife passed through the kitchen on her way from the dining-room, and went out into the garden and that she was carrying a knife.'

Tim stared at him.

'Molly, carrying a knife? Well, why shouldn't she? I mean—why—you don't think—what are you trying to suggest?'

'I am talking of the time before people had come into the dining-room. It would be, I suppose, some time about 8.30. You yourself were in the dining-room talking to the head waiter, Fernando, I believe.'

'Yes.' Tim cast his mind back. 'Yes, I remember.'

'And your wife came in from the terrace?'

'Yes, she did,' Tim agreed. 'She always went out to look

115

over the tables. Sometimes the boys set things wrong, forgot some of the cutlery, things like that. Very likely that's what it was. She may have been rearranging cutlery or something. She might have had a spare knife or a spoon, something like that in her hand.'

'And she came from the terrace into the dining-room. Did she speak to you?'

'Yes, we had a word or two together.'

'What did she say? Can you remember?'

'I think I asked her who she'd been talking to. I heard her voice out there.'

'And who did she say she'd been talking to?'

'Gregory Dyson.'

'Ah. Yes. That is what *he* said.'

Tim went on, 'He'd been making a pass at her, I understand. He was a bit given to that kind of thing. It annoyed me and I said "Blast him" and Molly laughed and said she could do all the blasting that needed to be done. Molly's a very clever girl that way. It's not always an easy position, you know. You can't offend guests, and so an attractive girl like Molly has to pass things off with a laugh and a shrug. Gregory Dyson finds it difficult to keep his hands off any good-looking woman.'

'Had there been an altercation between them?'

'No, I don't think so. I think, as I say, she just laughed it off as usual.'

'You can't say definitely whether she had a knife in her hand or not?'

'I can't remember—I'm almost sure she didn't—in fact quite sure she didn't.'

'But you said just now . . .'

'Look here, what I meant was that if she was in the dining-room or in the kitchen it's quite likely she might have picked up a knife or had one in her hand. Matter of fact I can remember quite well, she came in from the dining-room and she had *nothing* in her hand. Nothing at all. That's definite.'

'I see,' said Weston.

Tim looked at him uneasily.

'What on earth is this you're getting at? What did that damn' fool Enrico—Manuel—whoever it was—say?'

'He said your wife came out into the kitchen, that she looked upset, that she had a knife in her hand.'

'He's just dramatizing.'

'Did you have any further conversation with your wife during dinner or after?'

'No, I don't think I did really. Matter of fact I was rather busy.'

'Was your wife there in the dining-room during the meal?'

'I—oh—yes, we always move about among the guests and things like that. See how things are going on.'

'Did you speak to her at all?'

'No, I don't think I did . . . We're usually fairly busy. We don't always notice what the other one's doing and we certainly haven't got time to talk to each other.'

'Actually you don't remember speaking to her until she came up the steps three hours later, after finding the body?'

'It was an awful shock for her. It upset her terribly.'

117

Agatha Christie

'I know. A very unpleasant experience. How did she come to be walking along the beach path?'

'After the stress of dinner being served, she often does go for a turn. You know, get away from the guests for a minute or two, get a breather.'

'When she came back, I understand you were talking to Mrs Hillingdon.'

'Yes. Practically everyone else had gone to bed.'

'What was the subject of your conversation with Mrs Hillingdon?'

'Nothing particular. Why? What's she been saying?'

'So far she hasn't said anything. We haven't asked her.'

'We were just talking of this and that. Molly, and hotel running, and one thing and another.'

'And then—your wife came up the steps of the terrace and told you what had happened?'

'Yes.'

'There was blood on her hands?'

'Of course there was! She'd bent over the girl, tried to lift her, couldn't understand what had happened, what was the matter with her. Of course there was blood on her hands! Look here, what the hell are you suggesting? You *are* suggesting something?'

'Please calm down,' said Daventry. 'It's all a great strain on you I know, Tim, but we have to get the facts clear. I understand your wife hasn't been feeling very well lately?'

'Nonsense—she's all right. Major Palgrave's death upset her a bit. Naturally. She's a sensitive girl.'

'We shall have to ask her a few questions as soon as she's fit enough,' said Weston.

118

'Well, you can't now. The doctor gave her a sedative and said she wasn't to be disturbed. I won't have her upset and brow-beaten, d'you hear?'

'We're not going to do any brow-beating,' said Weston. 'We've just got to get the facts clear. We won't disturb her at present, but as soon as the doctor allows us, we'll have to see her.' His voice was gentle—inflexible.

Tim looked at him, opened his mouth, but said nothing.

Evelyn Hillingdon, calm and composed as usual, sat down in the chair indicated. She considered the few questions asked her, taking her time over it. Her dark, intelligent eyes looked at Weston thoughtfully.

'Yes,' she said, 'I was talking to Mr Kendal on the terrace when his wife came up the steps and told us about the murder.'

'Your husband wasn't there?'

'No, he had gone to bed.'

'Had you any special reason for your conversation with Mr Kendal?'

Evelyn raised her finely pencilled eyebrows—It was a definite rebuke.

She said coldly:

'What a very odd question. No—there was nothing special about our conversation.'

'Did you discuss the matter of his wife's health?'

Again Evelyn took her time.

'I really can't remember,' she said at last.

Agatha Christie

'Are you sure of that?'

'Sure that I can't remember? What a curious way of putting it—one talks about so many things at different times.'

'Mrs Kendal has not been in good health lately, I understand.'

'She looked quite all right—a little tired perhaps. Of course running a place like this means a lot of worries, and she is quite inexperienced. Naturally, she gets flustered now and then.'

'Flustered.' Weston repeated the word. 'That was the way you would describe it?'

'It's an old-fashioned word, perhaps, but just as good as the modern jargon we use for everything—A "virus infection" for a bilious attack—an "anxiety neurosis" for the minor bothers of daily life—'

Her smile made Weston feel slightly ridiculous. He thought to himself that Evelyn Hillingdon was a clever woman. He looked at Daventry, whose face remained unmoved, and wondered what he thought.

'Thank you, Mrs Hillingdon,' said Weston.

'We don't want to worry you, Mrs Kendal, but we have to have your account of just how you came to find this girl. Dr Graham says you are sufficiently recovered to talk about it now.'

'Oh yes,' said Molly, 'I'm really quite all right again.' She gave them a small nervous smile. 'It was just the shock—It *was* rather awful, you know.'

120

'Yes, indeed it must have been—I understand you went for a walk after dinner.'

'Yes—I often do.'

Her eyes shifted, Daventry noticed, and the fingers of her hands twined and untwined about each other.

'What time would that have been, Mrs Kendal?' asked Weston.

'Well, I don't really know—we don't go much by the time.'

'The steel band was still playing?'

'Yes—at least—I think so—I can't really remember.'

'And you walked—which way?'

'Oh, along the beach path.'

'To the left or the right?'

'Oh! First one way—and then the other—I—I—really didn't notice.'

'Why didn't you notice, Mrs Kendal?'

She frowned.

'I suppose I was—well—thinking of things.'

'Thinking of anything particular?'

'No—No—Nothing particular—Just things that had to be done—seen to—in the hotel.' Again that nervous twining and untwining of fingers. 'And then—I noticed something white—in a clump of hibiscus bushes—and I wondered what it was. I stopped and—and pulled—' She swallowed convulsively—'And it was her—Victoria—all huddled up—and I tried to raise her head up and I got—blood—on my hands.'

She looked at them and repeated wonderingly as though recalling something impossible:

'Blood—on my hands.'

'Yes—Yes—A very dreadful experience. There is no need for you to tell us more about that part of it—How long had you been walking, do you think, when you found her—'

'I don't know—I have no idea.'

'An hour? Half an hour? Or more than an hour—'

'I don't know,' Molly repeated.

Daventry asked in a quiet everyday voice:

'Did you take a knife with you on your—walk?'

'A knife?' Molly sounded surprised. 'Why should I take a knife?'

'I only ask because one of the kitchen staff mentioned that you had a knife in your hand when you went out of the kitchen into the garden.'

Molly frowned.

'But I didn't go out of the kitchen—oh you mean earlier—before dinner—I—I don't *think* so—'

'You had been rearranging the cutlery on the tables, perhaps.'

'I have to, sometimes. They lay things wrong—not enough knives—or too many. The wrong number of forks and spoons—that sort of thing.'

'So you may have gone out of the kitchen that evening carrying a knife in your hand?'

'I don't think I did—I'm sure I didn't—' She added— 'Tim was there—he would know. Ask him.'

'Did you like this girl—Victoria—was she good at her work?' asked Weston.

'Yes—she was a very nice girl.'

'You had no dispute with her?'

'Dispute? No.'

'She had never threatened you—in any way?'

'Threatened me? What do you mean?'

'It doesn't matter—You have no idea of who could have killed her? No idea at all?'

'None.' She spoke positively.

'Well, thank you, Mrs Kendal.' He smiled. 'It wasn't so terrible, was it?'

'That's all?'

'That's all for now.'

Daventry got up, opened the door for her, and watched her go out.

'Tim would know,' he quoted as he returned to his chair. 'And Tim says definitely that she *didn't* have a knife.'

Weston said gravely:

'I think that that is what any husband would feel called upon to say.'

'A table knife seems a very poor type of knife to use for murder.'

'But it was a *steak* knife, Mr Daventry. Steaks were on the menu that evening. Steak knives are kept sharp.'

'I really can't bring myself to believe that that girl we've just been talking to is a red-handed murderess, Weston.'

'It is not necessary to believe it yet. It could be that Mrs Kendal went out into the garden before dinner, clasping a knife she had taken off one of the tables because it was superfluous—she might not even have noticed she was holding it, and she could have put it down some-where—or dropped it—It could have been found and used by someone else—I, too, think her an unlikely murderess.'

'All the same,' said Daventry thoughtfully, 'I'm pretty sure she is not telling all she knows. Her vagueness over time is odd—where was she—what was she doing out there? Nobody, so far, seems to have noticed her in the dining-room that evening.'

'The husband was about as usual—but not the wife—'

'You think she went to meet someone—Victoria Johnson?'

'Perhaps—or perhaps she saw whoever it was who did go to meet Victoria.'

'You're thinking of Gregory Dyson?'

'We know he was talking to Victoria earlier—He may have arranged to meet her again later—everyone moved around freely on the terrace, remember—dancing, drinking—in and out of the bar.'

'No alibi like a steel band,' said Daventry wryly.

CHAPTER 16

Miss Marple Seeks Assistance

If anybody had been there to observe the gentle-looking elderly lady who stood meditatively on the loggia outside her bungalow, they would have thought she had nothing more on her mind than deliberation on how to arrange her time that day—An expedition, perhaps, to Castle Cliff—a visit to Jamestown—a nice drive and lunch at Pelican Point—or just a quiet morning on the beach—

But the gentle old lady was deliberating quite other matters—she was in militant mood.

'*Something has got to be done*,' said Miss Marple to herself.

Moreover, she was convinced that there was no time to be lost—There was urgency.

But who was there that she could convince of that fact? Given time, she thought she could find out the truth by herself.

She had found out a good deal. But not enough—not nearly enough. And time was short.

She realized, bitterly, that here on this Paradise of an island, she had none of her usual allies.

She thought regretfully of her friends in England—Sir Henry Clithering—always willing to listen indulgently—his godson Dermot, who in spite of his increased status at Scotland Yard was still ready to believe that when Miss Marple voiced an opinion there was usually something behind it.

But would that soft-voiced native police officer pay any attention to an old lady's urgency? Dr Graham? But Dr Graham was not what she needed—too gentle and hesitant, certainly not a man of quick decisions and rapid actions.

Miss Marple, feeling rather like a humble deputy of the Almighty, almost cried aloud her need in Biblical phrasing.

Who will go for me?

Whom shall I send?

The sound that reached her ears a moment later was not instantly recognized by her as an answer to prayer—far from it—At the back of her mind it registered only as a man possibly calling his dog.

'Hi!'

Miss Marple, lost in perplexity, paid no attention.

'Hi!' The volume thus increased, Miss Marple looked vaguely round.

'HI!' called Mr Rafiel impatiently. He added—'You there—'

Miss Marple had not at first realized that Mr Rafiel's 'Hi You' was addressed to her. It was not a method that

126

anyone had ever used before to summon her. It was certainly not a gentlemanly mode of address. Miss Marple did not resent it, because people seldom did resent Mr Rafiel's somewhat arbitrary method of doing things. He was a law unto himself and people accepted him as such. Miss Marple looked across the intervening space between her bungalow and his. Mr Rafiel was sitting outside on his loggia and he beckoned her.

'You were calling me?' she asked.

'Of course I was calling you,' said Mr Rafiel. 'Who did you think I was calling—a cat? Come over here.'

Miss Marple looked round for her handbag, picked it up, and crossed the intervening space.

'I can't come to you unless someone helps me,' explained Mr Rafiel, 'so you've got to come to me.'

'Oh yes,' said Miss Marple, 'I quite understand *that*.'

Mr Rafiel pointed to an adjacent chair. 'Sit down,' he said, 'I want to talk to you. Something damned odd is going on in this island.'

'Yes, indeed,' agreed Miss Marple, taking the chair as indicated. By sheer habit she drew her knitting out of her bag.

'Don't start knitting again,' said Mr Rafiel, 'I can't stand it. I hate women knitting. It irritates me.'

Miss Marple returned her knitting to her bag. She did this with no undue air of meekness, rather with the air of one who makes allowances for a fractious patient.

'There's a lot of chit-chat going on,' said Mr Rafiel, 'and I bet you're in the forefront of it. You and the parson and his sister.'

'It is, perhaps, only natural that there should be chit-chat,' said Miss Marple with spirit, 'given the circumstances.'

'This Island girl gets herself knifed. Found in the bushes. *Might* be ordinary enough. That chap she was living with might have got jealous of another man—or he'd got himself another girl and she got jealous and they had a row. Sex in the tropics. That sort of stuff. What do you say?'

'No,' said Miss Marple, shaking her head.

'The authorities don't think so, either.'

'They would say more to you,' pointed out Miss Marple, 'than they would say to me.'

'All the same, I bet you know more about it than I do. You've listened to the tittle-tattle.'

'Certainly I have,' said Miss Marple.

'Nothing much else to do, have you, except listen to tittle-tattle?'

'It is often informative and useful.'

'D'you know,' said Mr Rafiel, studying her attentively. 'I made a mistake about you. I don't often make mistakes about people. There's a lot more to you than I thought there was. All these rumours about Major Palgrave and the stories he told. You think he was bumped off, don't you?'

'I very much fear so,' said Miss Marple.

'Well, he was,' said Mr Rafiel.

Miss Marple drew a deep breath. 'That is definite, is it?' she asked.

'Yes, it's definite enough. I had it from Daventry. I'm

not breaking a confidence because the facts of the autopsy will have to come out. You told Graham something, he went to Daventry, Daventry went to the Administrator, the CID were informed, and between them they agreed that things looked fishy, so they dug up old Palgrave and had a look.'

'And they found?' Miss Marple paused interrogatively.

'They found he'd had a lethal dose of something that only a doctor could pronounce properly. As far as I remember it sounds vaguely like di-flor, hexagonal-ethylcarbenzol. That's not the right name. But that's roughly what it *sounds* like. The police doctor put it that way so that nobody should know, I suppose, what it really *was*. The stuff's probably got some quite simple nice easy name like Evipan or Veronal or Easton's Syrup or something of that kind. This is its official name to baffle laymen with. Anyway, a sizeable dose of it, I gather, would produce death, and the signs would be much the same as those of high blood pressure aggravated by over-indulgence in alcohol on a gay evening. In fact, it all looked perfectly natural and nobody questioned it for a moment. Just said "poor old chap" and buried him quick. Now they wonder if he ever had high blood pressure at all. Did he ever say he had to you?'

'No.'

'Exactly! And yet everyone seems to have taken it as a fact.'

'Apparently he told people he had.'

'It's like seeing ghosts,' said Mr Rafiel. 'You never meet the chap who's seen the ghost himself. It's always the second cousin of his aunt, or a friend, or a friend of a friend. But leave that for a moment. They thought he had blood pressure, because there was a bottle of tablets controlling blood pressure found in his room but—and now we're coming to the point—I gather that this girl who was killed went about saying that that bottle was put there by somebody else, and that *actually* it belonged to that fellow Greg.'

'Mr Dyson *has* got blood pressure. His wife mentioned it,' said Miss Marple.

'So it was put in Palgrave's room to suggest that he suffered from blood pressure and to make his death seem natural.'

'Exactly,' said Miss Marple. 'And the story was put about, very cleverly, that he had frequently mentioned to people that he had high blood pressure. But you know, it's very easy to put about a story. Very easy. I've seen a lot of it in my time.'

'I bet you have,' said Mr Rafiel.

'It only needs a murmur here and there,' said Miss Marple. 'You don't say it of your own knowledge, you just say that Mrs B. told you that Colonel C. told her. It's always at second hand or third hand or fourth hand and it's very difficult to find out who was the original whisperer. Oh yes, it can be done. And the people you say it to go on and repeat it to others as if they know it of their own knowledge.'

'Somebody's been clever,' said Mr Rafiel thoughtfully.

'Yes,' said Miss Marple, 'I think somebody's been quite clever.'

'This girl saw something, or knew something and tried blackmail, I suppose,' said Mr Rafiel.

'She mayn't have thought of it as blackmail,' said Miss Marple. 'In these large hotels, there are often things the maids know that some people would rather not have repeated. And so they hand out a larger tip or a little present of money. The girl possibly didn't realize at first the importance of what she knew.'

'Still, she got a knife in her back all right,' said Mr Rafiel brutally.

'Yes. Evidently someone couldn't afford to let her talk.'

'Well? Let's hear what you think about it all.'

Miss Marple looked at him thoughtfully.

'Why should you think I know any more than you do, Mr Rafiel?'

'Probably you don't,' said Mr Rafiel, 'but I'm interested to hear your ideas about what you do know.'

'But why?'

'There's not very much to do out here,' said Mr Rafiel, 'except make money.'

Miss Marple looked slightly surprised.

'Make money? Out here?'

'You can send out half a dozen cables in code every day if you like,' said Mr Rafiel. 'That's how I amuse myself.'

'Take-over bids?' Miss Marple asked doubtfully, in the tone of one who speaks a foreign language.

'That kind of thing,' agreed Mr Rafiel. 'Pitting your wits against other people's wits. The trouble is it doesn't occupy enough time, so I've got interested in this business.

Agatha Christie

It's aroused my curiosity. Palgrave spent a good deal of his time talking to you. Nobody else would be bothered with him, I expect. What did he say?'

'He told me a good many stories,' said Miss Marple.

'I know he did. Damn' boring, most of them. And you hadn't only got to hear them once. If you got anywhere within range you heard them three or four times over.'

'I know,' said Miss Marple. 'I'm afraid that does happen when gentlemen get older.'

Mr Rafiel looked at her very sharply.

'I don't tell stories,' he said. 'Go on. It started with one of Palgrave's stories, did it?'

'He said he knew a murderer,' said Miss Marple. 'There's nothing really special about that,' she added in her gentle voice, 'because I suppose it happens to nearly everybody.'

'I don't follow you,' said Mr Rafiel.

'I don't mean specifically,' said Miss Marple, 'but surely, Mr Rafiel, if you cast over in your mind your recollections of various events in your life, hasn't there nearly always been an occasion when somebody has made some careless reference such as "Oh yes I knew the So-and-So's quite well—he died very suddenly and they always say his wife did him in, but I dare say that's just gossip." You've heard people say something like that, haven't you?'

'Well, I suppose so—yes, something of the kind. But not—well, not seriously.'

'Exactly,' said Miss Marple, 'but Major Palgrave was a very serious man. I think he enjoyed telling this story. He said he had a snapshot of the murderer. He was going to show it to me but—actually—he didn't.'

132

'Why?'

'Because he saw something,' said Miss Marple. 'Saw someone, I suspect. His face got very red and he shoved back the snapshot into his wallet and began talking on another subject.'

'Who did he see?'

'I've thought about that a good deal,' said Miss Marple. 'I was sitting outside my bungalow, and he was sitting nearly opposite me and—whatever he saw, he saw over my right shoulder.'

'Someone coming along the path then from behind you on the right, the path from the creek and the car park—'

'Yes.'

'*Was* anyone coming along the path?'

'Mr and Mrs Dyson and Colonel and Mrs Hillingdon.'

'Anybody else?'

'Not that I can find out. Of course, your bungalow would also be in his line of vision . . .'

'Ah. Then we include—shall we say—Esther Walters and my chap, Jackson. Is that right? Either of them, I suppose, *might* have come out of the bungalow and gone back inside again without your seeing them.'

'They might have,' said Miss Marple, 'I didn't turn my head at once.'

'The Dysons, the Hillingdons, Esther, Jackson. One of them's a murderer. Or, of course, myself,' he added; obviously as an afterthought.

Miss Marple smiled faintly.

'And he spoke of the murderer as a *man*?'

'Yes.'

'Right. That cuts out Evelyn Hillingdon, Lucky and Esther Walters. So your murderer, allowing that all this far-fetched nonsense is true, your murderer is Dyson, Hillingdon or my smooth-tongued Jackson.'

'Or yourself,' said Miss Marple.

Mr Rafiel ignored this last point.

'Don't say things to irritate me,' he said. 'I'll tell you the first thing that strikes me, and which you don't seem to have thought of. *If* it's one of those three, why the devil didn't old Palgrave recognize him before? Dash it all, they've all been sitting round looking at each other for the last two weeks. That doesn't seem to make sense.'

'I think it could,' said Miss Marple.

'Well, tell me how.'

'You see, in Major Palgrave's story he hadn't seen this man *himself* at any time. It was a story told to him by a doctor. The doctor gave him the snapshot as a curiosity. Major Palgrave may have looked at the snapshot fairly closely at the time but after that he'd just stack it away in his wallet and keep it as a souvenir. Occasionally, perhaps, he'd take it out and show it to someone he was telling the story to. And another thing, Mr Rafiel, we don't know how long ago this happened. He didn't give me any indication of that when he was telling the story. I mean this may have been a story he's been telling to people for *years*. Five years—ten years—longer still perhaps. Some of his tiger stories go back about twenty years.'

'They would!' said Mr Rafiel.

'So I don't suppose for a moment that Major Palgrave

would recognize the face in the snapshot if he came across the man casually. What I think happened, what I'm almost sure *must* have happened, is that as he told his story he fumbled for the snapshot, took it out, looked down at it studying the face and then looked up to see *the same face*, or one with a strong resemblance, coming towards him from a distance of about ten or twelve feet away.'

'Yes,' said Mr Rafiel consideringly, 'yes, that's possible.'

'He was taken aback,' said Miss Marple, 'and he shoved it back in his wallet and began to talk loudly about something else.'

'He couldn't have been sure,' said Mr Rafiel, shrewdly.

'No,' said Miss Marple, 'he couldn't have been sure. But of course afterwards he would have studied the snapshot very carefully and would have looked at the man and tried to make up his mind whether it was just a likeness or whether it could actually be the same person.'

Mr Rafiel reflected a moment or two, then he shook his head.

'There's something wrong here. The motive's inadequate. Absolutely inadequate. He was speaking to you loudly, was he?'

'Yes,' said Miss Marple, 'quite loudly. He always did.'

'True enough. Yes, he did shout. So whoever was approaching would hear what he said?'

'I should imagine you could hear it for quite a good radius round.'

Mr Rafiel shook his head again. He said, 'It's fantastic, too fantastic. Anybody would laugh at such a story. Here's an old booby telling a story about another story somebody told him, and showing a snapshot, and all of it centring round a murder which had taken place years ago! Or at any rate, a year or two. How on earth can *that* worry the man in question? No evidence, just a bit of hearsay, a story at third hand. He could even admit a likeness, he could say: "Yes, I *do* look rather like that fellow, don't I! Ha, ha!" Nobody's going to take old Palgrave's identification seriously. Don't tell me so, because I won't believe it. No, the chap, if it *was* the chap, had nothing to fear—nothing whatever. It's the kind of accusation he can just laugh off. Why on earth should he proceed to murder old Palgrave? It's absolutely unnecessary. You must see that.'

'Oh I do see that,' said Miss Marple. 'I couldn't agree with you more. That's what makes me uneasy. So very uneasy that I really couldn't sleep last night.'

Mr Rafiel stared at her. 'Let's hear what's on your mind,' he said quietly.

'I may be entirely wrong,' said Miss Marple hesitantly.

'Probably you are,' said Mr Rafiel with his usual lack of courtesy, 'but at any rate let's hear what you've thought up in the small hours.'

'There could be a very powerful motive if—'

'If what?'

'If there was going to be—quite soon—*another murder*.'

Mr Rafiel stared at her. He tried to pull himself up a little in his chair.

'Let's get this clear,' he said.

'I am so bad at explaining.' Miss Marple spoke rapidly and rather incoherently. A pink flush rose to her cheeks.

'Supposing there was a murder planned. If you remember, the story Major Palgrave told me concerned a man whose wife died under suspicious circumstances. Then, after a certain lapse of time, there was another murder under exactly the same circumstances. A man of a different name had a wife who died in much the same way and the doctor who was telling it recognized him as the same man, although he'd changed his name. Well, it does look, doesn't it, as though this murderer might be the kind of murderer who made a habit of the thing?'

'You mean like Smith, Brides in the Bath, that kind of thing. Yes.'

'As far as I can make out,' said Miss Marple, 'and from what I have heard and read, a man who does a wicked thing like this and gets away with it the first time, is, alas, *encouraged*. He thinks it's easy, he thinks he's clever. And so he repeats it. And in the end, as you say, like Smith and the Brides in the Bath, it becomes a *habit*. Each time in a different place and each time the man changes his name. But the crimes themselves are all very much alike. So it seems to me, although I may be quite wrong—'

'But you don't think you are wrong, do you?' Mr Rafiel put in shrewdly.

Miss Marple went on without answering. '—that if that *were* so and if this—this person had got things all lined up for a murder out here, for getting rid of *another* wife, say, and if this is crime three or four, well then, the Major's story *would* matter because the murderer couldn't afford to have any similarity pointed out. If you remember, that was exactly the way Smith got caught. The circumstances

Agatha Christie

of a crime attracted the attention of somebody who compared it with a newspaper clipping of some other case. So you do see, don't you, that if this wicked person has got a crime planned, arranged, and shortly about to take place, he couldn't afford to let Major Palgrave go about telling this story and showing that snapshot.'

She stopped and looked appealingly at Mr Rafiel.

'So you see he had to do something very quickly, as quickly as possible.'

Mr Rafiel spoke. 'In fact, that very same night, eh?'

'Yes,' said Miss Marple.

'Quick work,' said Mr Rafiel, 'but it could be done. Put the tablets in old Palgrave's room, spread the blood pressure rumour about and add a little of our fourteen-syllable drug to a Planters Punch. Is that it?'

'Yes—But that's all over—we needn't worry about it. It's the _future_. It's now. With Major Palgrave out of the way and the snapshot destroyed, _this man will go on with his murder as planned_.'

Mr Rafiel whistled.

'You've got it all worked out, haven't you?'

Miss Marple nodded. She said in a most unaccustomed voice, firm and almost dictatorial, 'And we've got to stop it. _You've_ got to stop it, Mr Rafiel.'

'Me?' said Mr Rafiel, astonished, 'Why me?'

'Because you're rich and important,' said Miss Marple, simply. 'People will take notice of what you say or suggest. They wouldn't listen to me for a moment. They would say that I was an old lady imagining things.'

'They might at that,' said Mr Rafiel. 'More fools if they

138

did. I must say, though, that nobody would think you had any brains in your head to hear your usual line of talk. Actually, you've got a logical mind. Very few women have.' He shifted himself uncomfortably in his chair. 'Where the hell's Esther or Jackson?' he said. 'I need resettling. No, it's no good your doing it. You're not strong enough. I don't know what they mean, leaving me alone like this.'

'I'll go and find them.'

'No, you won't. You'll stay here—and thrash this out. Which of them is it? The egregious Greg? The quiet Edward Hillingdon or my fellow Jackson? It's got to be one of the three, hasn't it?'

CHAPTER 17

Mr Rafiel Takes Charge

'I don't know,' said Miss Marple.

'What do you mean? What have we been talking about for the last twenty minutes?'

'It has occurred to me that I may have been wrong.'

Mr Rafiel stared at her.

'Scatty after all!' he said disgustedly. 'And you sounded so sure of yourself.'

'Oh, I am sure—about the *murder*. It's the *murderer* I'm not sure about. You see I've found out that Major Palgrave had more than one murder story—you told me yourself he'd told you one about a kind of Lucrezia Borgia—'

'So he did—at that. But that was quite a different kind of story.'

'I know. And Mrs Walters said he had one about someone being gassed in a gas oven—'

'But the story he told you—'

Miss Marple allowed herself to interrupt—a thing that did not often happen to Mr Rafiel.

140

She spoke with desperate earnestness and only moderate incoherence.

'Don't you see—it's so difficult to be *sure*. The whole point is that—so often—one doesn't *listen*. Ask Mrs Walters—she said the same thing—you listen to begin with—and then your attention flags—your mind wanders—and suddenly you find you've missed a bit. I just wonder if possibly there may have been a gap—a very small one—between the story he was telling me—about a *man*—and the moment when he was getting out his wallet and saying—"Like to see a picture of a murderer."'

'But you thought it was a picture of the man he had been talking about?'

'I thought so—yes. It never occurred to me that it mightn't have been. But now—how can I be *sure*?'

Mr Rafiel looked at her very thoughtfully . . .

'The trouble with you is,' he said, 'that you're too conscientious. Great mistake—Make up your mind and don't shilly shally. You didn't shilly shally to begin with. If you ask me, in all this chit-chat you've been having with the parson's sister and the rest of them, you've got hold of something that's unsettled you.'

'Perhaps you're right.'

'Well, cut it out for the moment. Let's go ahead with what you had to begin with. Because, nine times out of ten, one's original judgments are right—or so I've found. We've got three suspects. Let's take 'em out and have a good look at them. Any preference?'

'I really haven't,' said Miss Marple, 'all three of them seem so very unlikely.'

'We'll take Greg first,' said Mr Rafiel. 'Can't stand the fellow. Doesn't make him a murderer, though. Still, there *are* one or two points against him. Those blood pressure tablets belonged to him. Nice and handy to make use of.'

'That would be a little obvious, wouldn't it?' Miss Marple objected.

'I don't know that it would,' said Mr Rafiel. 'After all, the main thing was to do something *quickly*, and he'd got the tablets. Hadn't much time to go looking round for tablets that somebody else might have. Let's say it's Greg. All right. *If* he wanted to put his dear wife Lucky out of the way—(Good job, too, I'd say. In fact I'm in sympathy with him.) I can't actually see his motive. From all accounts he's rich. Inherited money from his first wife who had pots of it. He qualifies on that as a possible wife murderer all right. But that's over and done with. He got away with it. But Lucky was his first wife's poor relation. No money there, so if he wants to put *her* out of the way it must be in order to marry somebody else. Any gossip going around about that?'

Miss Marple shook her head.

'Not that I have heard. He—er—has a very gallant manner with *all* the ladies.'

'Well, that's a nice, old-fashioned way of putting it,' said Mr Rafiel. 'All right, he's a stoat. He makes passes. Not enough! We want more than that. Let's go on to Edward Hillingdon. Now there's a dark horse, if ever there was one.'

'He is not, I think, a happy man,' offered Miss Marple.

Mr Rafiel looked at her thoughtfully.

'Do you think a murderer ought to be a happy man?' Miss Marple coughed.

'Well, they usually have been in my experience.'

'I don't suppose your experience has gone very far,' said Mr Rafiel.

In this assumption, as Miss Marple could have told him, he was wrong. But she forbore to contest his statement. Gentlemen, she knew, did not like to be put right in their facts.

'I rather fancy Hillingdon myself,' said Mr Rafiel. 'I've an idea that there is something a bit odd going on between him and his wife. You noticed it at all?'

'Oh yes,' said Miss Marple, 'I have noticed it. Their behaviour is perfect in public, of course, but that one would expect.'

'You probably know more about those sort of people than I would,' said Mr Rafiel. 'Very well, then, everything is in perfectly good taste but it's a probability that, in a gentlemanly way, Edward Hillingdon is contemplating doing away with Evelyn Hillingdon. Do you agree?'

'If so,' said Miss Marple, 'there must be another woman.'

'But what woman?'

Miss Marple shook her head in a dissatisfied manner.

'I can't help feeling—I really can't—that it's not all quite as simple as that.'

'Well, who shall we consider next—Jackson? We leave me out of it.'

Miss Marple smiled for the first time.

'And why do we leave you out of it, Mr Rafiel?'

'Because if you want to discuss the possibilities of my being a murderer you'd have to do it with somebody else. Waste of time talking about it to me. And anyway, I ask you, am I cut out for the part? Helpless, hauled out of bed like a dummy, dressed, wheeled about in a chair, shuffled along for a walk. What earthly chance have *I* of going and murdering anyone?'

'Probably as good a chance as anyone else,' said Miss Marple vigorously.

'And how do you make that out?'

'Well, you would agree yourself, I think, that you have brains?'

'Of course I've got brains,' declared Mr Rafiel. 'A good deal more than anybody else in this community, I'd say.'

'And having brains,' went on Miss Marple, 'would enable you to overcome the physical difficulties of being a murderer.'

'It would take some doing!'

'Yes,' said Miss Marple, 'it would take some doing. But then, I think, Mr Rafiel, you would enjoy that.'

Mr Rafiel stared at her for a long time and then he suddenly laughed.

'You've got a nerve!' he said. 'Not quite the gentle fluffy old lady you look, are you? So you really think I'm a murderer?'

'No,' said Miss Marple, 'I do not.'

'And why?'

'Well, really, I think just *because* you have got brains. Having brains, you can get most things you want without

144

having recourse to murder. Murder is stupid.'

'And anyway who the devil should I want to murder?'

'That would be a very interesting question,' said Miss Marple. 'I have not yet had the pleasure of sufficient conversation with you to evolve a theory as to that.'

Mr Rafiel's smile broadened.

'Conversations with you might be dangerous,' he said.

'Conversations are always dangerous, if you have something to hide,' said Miss Marple.

'You may be right. Let's get on to Jackson. What do you think of Jackson?'

'It is difficult for me to say. I have not had the opportunity really of *any* conversation with him.'

'So you've no views on the subject?'

'He reminds me a little,' said Miss Marple reflectively, 'of a young man in the Town Clerk's office near where I live, Jonas Parry.'

'And?' Mr Rafiel asked and paused.

'He was not,' said Miss Marple, 'very satisfactory.'

'Jackson's not wholly satisfactory either. He suits me all right. He's first class at his job, and he doesn't mind being sworn at. He knows he's damn' well paid and so he puts up with things. I wouldn't employ him in a position of trust, but I don't have to trust him. Maybe his past is blameless, maybe it isn't. His references were all right but I discern—shall I say—a note of reserve. Fortunately, I'm not a man who has any guilty secrets, so I'm not a subject for blackmail.'

'No secrets?' said Miss Marple, thoughtfully. 'Surely, Mr Rafiel, you have business secrets?'

'Not where Jackson can get at them. No. Jackson is a smooth article, one might say, but I really don't see him as a murderer. I'd say that wasn't his line at all.'

He paused a minute and then said suddenly, 'Do you know, if one stands back and takes a good look at all this fantastic business, Major Palgrave and his ridiculous stories and all the rest of it, the *emphasis* is entirely wrong. *I'm* the person who ought to be murdered.'

Miss Marple looked at him in some surprise.

'Proper type casting,' explained Mr Rafiel. 'Who's the victim in murder stories? Elderly men with lots of money.'

'And lots of people with a good reason for wishing him out of the way, so as to get that money,' said Miss Marple. 'Is that true also?'

'Well—' Mr Rafiel considered. 'I can count up to five or six men in London who wouldn't burst into tears if they read my obituary in *The Times*. But they wouldn't go so far as to do anything to bring about my demise. After all, why should they? I'm expected to die any day. In fact the bug—blighters are astonished that I've lasted so long. The doctors are surprised too.'

'You have, of course, a great will to live,' said Miss Marple.

'You think that's odd, I suppose,' said Mr Rafiel.

Miss Marple shook her head.

'Oh no,' she said, 'I think it's quite natural. Life is more worth living, more full of interest when you are likely to lose it. It shouldn't be, perhaps, but it is. When you're young and strong and healthy, and life stretches ahead of you, living isn't really important at all. It's young people

146

who commit suicide easily, out of despair from love, sometimes from sheer anxiety and worry. But old people know how valuable life is and how interesting.'

'Hah!' said Mr Rafiel, snorting. 'Listen to a couple of old crocks.'

'Well, what I said is true, isn't it?' demanded Miss Marple.

'Oh, yes,' said Mr Rafiel, 'it's true enough. But don't you think I'm right when I say that I ought to be cast as the victim?'

'It depends on who has reason to gain by your death,' said Miss Marple.

'Nobody, really,' said Mr Rafiel. 'Apart, as I've said, from my competitors in the business world who, as I have also said, can count comfortably on my being out of it before very long. I'm not such a fool as to leave a lot of money divided up among my relations. Precious little they'd get of it after the Government had taken practically the lot. Oh, no, I've attended to all that years ago. Settlements, trusts and all the rest of it.'

'Jackson, for instance, wouldn't profit by your death?'

'He wouldn't get a penny,' said Mr Rafiel cheerfully. 'I pay him double the salary that he'd get from anyone else. That's because he has to put up with my bad temper; and he knows quite well that he will be the loser when I die.'

'And Mrs Walters?'

'The same goes for Esther. She's a good girl. First-class secretary, intelligent, good-tempered, understands my ways, doesn't turn a hair if I fly off the handle, couldn't

147

care less if I insult her. Behaves like a nice nursery governess in charge of an outrageous and obstreperous child. She irritates me a bit sometimes, but who doesn't? There's nothing outstanding about her. She's rather a commonplace young woman in many ways, but I couldn't have anyone who suited me better. She's had a lot of trouble in her life. Married a man who wasn't much good. I'd say she never had much judgment when it came to men. Some women haven't. They fall for anyone who tells them a hard-luck story. Always convinced that all the man needs is proper female understanding. That, once married to her, he'll pull up his socks and make a go of life! But of course that type of man never does. Anyway, fortunately her unsatisfactory husband died; drank too much at a party one night and stepped in front of a bus. Esther had a daughter to support and she went back to her secretarial job. She's been with me five years. I made it quite clear to her from the start that she need have no expectations from me in the event of my death. I paid her from the start a very large salary, and that salary I've augmented by as much as a quarter as much again each year. However decent and honest people are, one should never trust *anybody*—that's why I told Esther quite clearly that she'd nothing to hope for from my death. Every year I live she'll get a bigger salary. If she puts most of that aside every year—and that's what I think she has done—she'll be quite a well-to-do woman by the time I kick the bucket. I've made myself responsible for her daughter's schooling and I've put a sum in trust for the daughter which she'll get when she comes of age. So Mrs Esther Walters is very comfortably placed. My death, let me tell you, would mean a serious financial loss to her.' He looked very hard at Miss Marple. 'She fully realizes all that. She's very sensible, Esther is.'

'Do she and Jackson get on?' asked Miss Marple.

Mr Rafiel shot a quick glance at her.

'Noticed something, have you?' he said. 'Yes, I think Jackson's done a bit of tom-catting around, with an eye in her direction, especially lately. He's a good-looking chap, of course, but he hasn't cut any ice in that direction. For one thing, there's class distinction. She's just a cut above him. Not very much. If she was *really* a cut above him it wouldn't matter, but the lower middle class—they're very particular. Her mother was a school teacher and her father a bank clerk. No, she won't make a fool of herself about Jackson. Dare say he's after her little nest egg, but he won't get it.'

'Hush—she's coming now!' said Miss Marple.

They both looked at Esther Walters as she came along the hotel path towards them.

'She's quite a good-looking girl, you know,' said Mr Rafiel, 'but not an atom of glamour. I don't know why, she's quite nicely turned out.'

Miss Marple sighed, a sigh that any woman will give however old at what might be considered wasted opportunities. What was lacking in Esther had been called by so many names during Miss Marple's span of existence. 'Not really attractive to me.' 'No SA.' 'Lacks Come-hither in her eye.' Fair hair, good complexion, hazel eyes, quite a good figure, pleasant smile, but lacking that something that makes a man's head turn when he passes a woman in the street.

'She ought to get married again,' said Miss Marple, lowering her voice.

'Of course she ought. She'd make a man a good wife.'

Esther Walters joined them and Mr Rafiel said, in a slightly artificial voice:

'So there you are at last! What's been keeping you?'

'Everyone seemed to be sending cables this morning,' said Esther. 'What with that, and people trying to check out—'

'Trying to check out, are they? A result of this murder business?'

'I suppose so. Poor Tim Kendal is worried to death.'

'And well he might be. Bad luck for that young couple, I must say.'

'I know. I gather it was rather a big undertaking for them to take on this place. They've been worried about making a success of it. They were doing very well, too.'

'They were doing a good job,' agreed Mr Rafiel. 'He's very capable and a damned hard worker. She's a very nice girl—attractive too. They've both worked like blacks, though that's an odd term to use out here, for blacks don't work themselves to death at all, so far as I can see. Was looking at a fellow shinning up a coconut tree to get his breakfast, then he goes to sleep for the rest of the day. Nice life.'

He added, 'We've been discussing the murder here.'

Esther Walters looked slightly startled. She turned her head towards Miss Marple.

'I've been wrong about her,' said Mr Rafiel, with characteristic frankness. 'Never been much of a one for the old pussies. All knitting wool and tittle-tattle. But this one's got something. Eyes and ears, and she uses them.'

Esther Walters looked apologetically at Miss Marple, but Miss Marple did not appear to take offence.

'That's really meant to be a compliment, you know,' Esther explained.

'I quite realize that,' said Miss Marple. 'I realize, too, that Mr Rafiel is privileged, or thinks he is.'

'What do you mean—privileged?' asked Mr Rafiel.

'To be rude if you want to be rude,' said Miss Marple.

'Have I been rude?' said Mr Rafiel, surprised. 'I'm sorry if I've offended you.'

'You haven't offended me,' said Miss Marple, 'I make allowances.'

'Now, don't be nasty. Esther, get a chair and bring it here. Maybe you can help.'

Esther walked a few steps to the balcony of the bungalow and brought over a light basket chair.

'We'll go on with our consultation,' said Mr Rafiel. 'We started with old Palgrave, deceased, and his eternal stories.'

'Oh, dear,' sighed Esther. 'I'm afraid I used to escape from him whenever I could.'

'Miss Marple was more patient,' said Mr Rafiel. 'Tell me, Esther, did he ever tell you a story about a murderer?'

'Oh yes,' said Esther. 'Several times.'

'What was it exactly? Let's have *your* recollection.'

'Well—' Esther paused to think. 'The trouble is,' she

said apologetically, 'I didn't really listen very closely. You see, it was rather like that terrible story about the lion in Rhodesia which used to go on and on. One did get rather in the habit of not listening.'

'Well, tell us what you *do* remember.'

'I think it arose out of some murder case that had been in the papers. Major Palgrave said that he'd had an experience not every person had had. He'd actually met a murderer face to face.'

'Met?' Mr Rafiel exclaimed. 'Did he actually use the word "met"?'

Esther looked confused.

'I think so.' She was doubtful. 'Or he may have said, "I can point you out a murderer."'

'Well, which was it? There's a difference.'

'I can't really be sure . . . I *think* he said he'd show me a picture of someone.'

'That's better.'

'And then he talked a lot about Lucrezia Borgia.'

'Never mind Lucrezia Borgia. We know all about her.'

'He talked about poisoners and that Lucrezia was very beautiful and had red hair. He said there were probably far more women poisoners going about the world than anyone knew.'

'That I fear is *quite* likely,' said Miss Marple.

'And he talked about poison being a woman's weapon.'

'Seems to have been wandering from the point a bit,' said Mr Rafiel.

'Well, of course, he always did wander from the point in his stories. And then one used to stop listening and just say "Yes" and "Really?" And "You don't say so".'

'What about this picture he was going to show you?'

'I don't remember. It may have been something he'd seen in the paper—'

'He didn't actually show you a snapshot?'

'A snapshot? No.' She shook her head. 'I'm quite sure of that. He did say that she was a good-looking woman, and you'd never think she was a murderer to look at her.'

'She?'

'There you are,' exclaimed Miss Marple. 'It makes it all so confusing.'

'He was talking about a woman?' Mr Rafiel asked.

'Oh, yes.'

'The snapshot was a snapshot of a woman?'

'Yes.'

'It can't have been!'

'But it was,' Esther persisted. 'He said "She's here in this island. I'll point her out to you, and then I'll tell you the whole story."'

Mr Rafiel swore. In saying what he thought of the late Major Palgrave he did not mince his words.

'The probabilities are,' he finished, 'that not a word of anything he said was true!'

'One does begin to wonder,' Miss Marple murmured.

'So there we are,' said Mr Rafiel. 'The old booby started telling you hunting tales. Pig sticking, tiger shooting, elephant hunting, narrow escapes from lions. One or two of them might have been fact. Several of them were fiction, and others had happened to somebody else! Then he gets on to the subject of murder and he tells one murder story to cap another murder story. And what's more he tells them all as if they'd happened to *him*. Ten to one most of them were a hash-up of what he'd read in the paper, or seen on TV.'

He turned accusingly on Esther. 'You admit that you weren't listening closely. Perhaps you misunderstood what he was saying.'

'I'm certain he was talking about a woman,' said Esther obstinately, 'because of course I wondered who it was.'

'Who do you think it was?' asked Miss Marple.

Esther flushed and looked slightly embarrassed.

'Oh, I didn't really—I mean, I wouldn't like to—'

Miss Marple did not insist. The presence of Mr Rafiel, she thought, was inimical to her finding out exactly what suppositions Esther Walters had made. That could only be cosily brought out in a tête-à-tête between two women. And there was, of course, the possibility that Esther Walters was lying. Naturally, Miss Marple did not suggest this aloud. She registered it as a possibility but she was not inclined to believe in it. For one thing she did not think that Esther Walters was a liar (though one never knew) and for another, she could see no point in such a lie.

'But *you* say,' Mr Rafiel was now turning upon Miss Marple, '*you* say that he told you this yarn about a murderer and that he then said he had a picture of him which he was going to show you.'

'I thought so, yes.'

'You thought so? You were sure enough to begin with!' Miss Marple retorted with spirit.

'It is never easy to repeat a conversation and be entirely

accurate in what the other party to it has said. One is always inclined to jump at what you think they *meant*. Then, afterwards, you put actual words into their mouths. Major Palgrave told me this story, yes. He told me that the man who told it to him, this doctor, had shown him a snapshot of the murderer; but if I am to be quite honest I must admit that what he actually said to me was "Would you like to see a snapshot of a murderer?" and naturally I assumed that it was the same snapshot he had been talking about. That it was the snapshot of that particular murderer. But I have to admit that it is possible—only remotely possible, but still possible—that by an association of ideas in his mind he leaped from the snapshot he had been shown in the past, to a snapshot he had taken recently of someone here who he was convinced was a murderer.'

'Women!' snorted Mr Rafiel in exasperation. 'You're all the same, the whole blinking lot of you! Can't be accurate. You're never exactly *sure* of what a thing was. And now,' he added irritably, 'where does *that* leave us?' He snorted. 'Evelyn Hillingdon, or Greg's wife, Lucky? The whole thing is a mess.'

There was a slight apologetic cough. Arthur Jackson was standing at Mr Rafiel's elbow. He had come so noiselessly that nobody had noticed him.

'Time for your massage, sir,' he said.

Mr Rafiel displayed immediate temper.

'What do you mean by sneaking up on me in that way and making me jump? I never heard you.'

'Very sorry, sir.'

155

'I don't think I'll have any massage today. It never does me a damn' bit of good.'

'Oh, come sir, you mustn't say that.' Jackson was full of professional cheerfulness. 'You'd soon notice if you left it off.'

He wheeled the chair deftly round.

Miss Marple rose to her feet, smiled at Esther and went down to the beach.

CHAPTER 18

Without Benefit of Clergy

The beach was rather empty this morning. Greg was
splashing in the water in his usual noisy style, Lucky
was lying on her face on the beach with a sun-tanned
back well oiled and her blonde hair splayed over her
shoulders. The Hillingdons were not there. Señora de
Caspearo, with an assorted bag of gentlemen in attendance, was lying face upwards and talking deep-throated,
happy Spanish. Some French and Italian children were
playing at the water's edge and laughing. Canon and Miss
Prescott were sitting in beach chairs observing the scene.
The Canon had his hat tilted forward over his eyes and
seemed half asleep. There was a convenient chair next to
Miss Prescott and Miss Marple made for it and sat down.

'Oh dear,' she said with a deep sigh.

'I know,' said Miss Prescott.

It was their joint tribute to violent death.

'That poor girl,' said Miss Marple.

'Very sad,' said the Canon. 'Most deplorable.'

'For a moment or two,' said Miss Prescott, 'we really

thought of leaving, Jeremy and I. But then we decided against it. It would not really be fair, I felt, on the Kendals. After all, it's not *their* fault—It might have happened anywhere.'

'In the midst of life we are in death,' said the Canon solemnly.

'It's very important, you know,' said Miss Prescott, 'that they should make a go of this place. They have sunk all their capital in it.'

'A very sweet girl,' said Miss Marple, 'but not looking at all well lately.'

'Very nervy,' agreed Miss Prescott. 'Of course her family—' she shook her head.

'I really think, Joan,' said the Canon in mild reproof, 'that there are some things—'

'Everybody knows about it,' said Miss Prescott. 'Her family live in our part of the world. A great-aunt—most peculiar—and one of her uncles took off all his clothes in one of the tube stations. Green Park, I believe it was.'

'Joan, that is a thing that should *not* be repeated.'

'Very sad,' said Miss Marple, shaking her head, 'though I believe not an uncommon form of madness. I know when we were working for the Armenian relief, a most respectable elderly clergyman was afflicted the same way. They telephoned his wife and she came along at once and took him home in a cab, wrapped in a blanket.'

'Of course, Molly's immediate family's all right,' said Miss Prescott. 'She never got on very well with her mother, but then so few girls seem to get on with their mothers nowadays.'

'Such a pity,' said Miss Marple, shaking her head, 'because really a young girl needs her mother's knowledge of the world and experience.'

'Exactly,' said Miss Prescott with emphasis. 'Molly, you know, took up with some man—*quite* unsuitable, I understand.'

'It so often happens,' said Miss Marple.

'Her family disapproved, naturally. *She* didn't tell them about it. They heard about it from a complete outsider. Of course her mother said she must bring him along so that they met him properly. This, I understand, the girl refused to do. She said it was humiliating to him. Most insulting to be made to come and meet her family and be looked over. Just as though you were a horse, she said.'

Miss Marple sighed. 'One does need so much *tact* when dealing with the young,' she murmured.

'Anyway, there it was! They forbade her to see him.'

'But you can't *do* that nowadays,' said Miss Marple. 'Girls have jobs and they meet people whether anyone forbids them or not.'

'But then, very fortunately,' went on Miss Prescott, 'she met Tim Kendal, and the other man sort of faded out of the picture. I can't *tell* you how relieved the family was.'

'I hope they didn't show it too plainly,' said Miss Marple. 'That so often puts girls off from forming suitable attachments.'

'Yes, indeed.'

'One remembers oneself—' murmured Miss Marple, her mind going back to the past. A young man she had met at a croquet party. He had seemed so nice—rather gay, almost *Bohemian* in his views. And then he had been unexpectedly warmly welcomed by her father. He had been suitable, eligible; he had been asked freely to the house more than once, and Miss Marple had found that, after all, he was *dull*. Very dull.

The Canon seemed safely comatose and Miss Marple advanced tentatively to the subject she was anxious to pursue.

'Of course you know so much about this place,' she murmured. 'You have been here several years running, have you not?'

'Well, last year and two years before that. We like St Honoré very much. Always such nice people here. Not the flashy, ultra-rich set.'

'So I suppose you know the Hillingdons and the Dysons well?'

'Yes, fairly well.'

Miss Marple coughed and lowered her voice slightly.

'Major Palgrave told me such an interesting story,' she said.

'He had a great repertoire of stories, hadn't he? Of course he had travelled very widely. Africa, India, even China I believe.'

'Yes indeed,' said Miss Marple. 'But I didn't mean one of *those* stories. This was a story concerned with—well, with one of the people I have just mentioned.'

'Oh!' said Miss Prescott. Her voice held meaning.

'Yes. Now I wonder—' Miss Marple allowed her eyes to travel gently round the beach to where Lucky lay sunning her back. 'Very beautifully tanned, isn't she,' remarked Miss Marple. 'And her hair. Most attractive. Practically the same colour as Molly Kendal's, isn't it?'

'The only difference,' said Miss Prescott, 'is that Molly's is natural and Lucky's comes out of a bottle!'

'Really, Joan,' the Canon protested, unexpectedly awake again. 'Don't you think that is *rather* an uncharitable thing to say?'

'It's not uncharitable,' said Miss Prescott, acidly. 'Merely a *fact*.'

'It looks very nice to *me*,' said the Canon.

'Of course. That's why she does it. But I assure you, my dear Jeremy, it wouldn't deceive any *woman* for a moment. Would it?' She appealed to Miss Marple.

'Well, I'm afraid—' said Miss Marple, 'of course I haven't the experience that you have—but I'm afraid—yes I should say definitely *not natural*. The appearance at the roots every fifth or sixth day—' She looked at Miss Prescott and they both nodded with quiet female assurance.

The Canon appeared to be dropping off again.

'Major Palgrave told me a really extraordinary story,' murmured Miss Marple, 'about—well I couldn't quite make out. I am a little deaf sometimes. He appeared to be saying or hinting—' she paused.

'I know what you mean. There was a great deal of talk at the time—'

'You mean at the time that—'

'When the first Mrs Dyson died. Her death was quite unexpected. In fact, everybody thought she was a *malade imaginaire*—a hypochondriac. So when she had the attack and died so unexpectedly, well, of course, people did talk.'

'There wasn't—any—trouble at the time?'

'The doctor was puzzled. He was quite a young man and he hadn't had much experience. He was what I call one of those antibiotics-for-all men. You know, the kind that doesn't bother to look at the patient much, or worry what's the matter with him. They just give them some kind of pill out of a bottle and if they don't get better, then they try a different pill. Yes, I believe he *was* puzzled, but it seemed she had had gastric trouble before. At least her husband said so, and there seemed no reason for believing anything was *wrong*.'

'But you yourself think—'

'Well, I always try to keep an open mind, but one does wonder, you know. And what with various things people said—'

'Joan!' The Canon sat up. He looked belligerent. 'I don't like—I really don't like to hear this kind of ill-natured gossip being repeated. We've always set our faces against that kind of thing. See no evil, hear no evil, speak no evil—and what is more, *think* no evil! That should be the motto of every Christian man and woman.'

The two women sat in silence. They were rebuked, and in deference to their training they deferred to the criticism of a man. But inwardly they were frustrated, irritated and quite unrepentant. Miss Prescott threw a frank glance of irritation towards her brother. Miss Marple took out her knitting and looked at it. Fortunately for them Chance was on their side.

'*Mon père*,' said a small shrill voice. It was one of the French children who had been playing at the water's edge.

162

She had come up unnoticed, and was standing by Canon Prescott's chair.

'*Mon père*,' she fluted.

'Eh? Yes, my dear? *Oui, qu'est-ce qu'il y a, ma petite?*'

The child explained. There had been a dispute about who should have the water-wings next and also other matters of seaside etiquette. Canon Prescott was extremely fond of children, especially small girls. He was always delighted to be summoned to act as arbiter in their disputes. He rose willingly now and accompanied the child to the water's edge. Miss Marple and Miss Prescott breathed deep sighs and turned avidly towards each other.

'Jeremy, of course rightly, is very against ill-natured gossip,' said Miss Prescott, 'but one cannot really ignore what people are saying. And there was, as I say, a great deal of talk at the time.'

'Yes?' Miss Marple's tone urged her forward.

'This young woman, you see, Miss Greatorex I think her name was then, I can't remember now, was a kind of cousin and she looked after Mrs Dyson. Gave her all her medicines and things like that.' There was a short, meaningless pause. 'And of course there had, I understand'—Miss Prescott's voice was lowered—'been goings-on between Mr Dyson and Miss Greatorex. A lot of people had noticed them. I mean things like that are quickly observed in a place like this. Then there was some curious story about some stuff that Edward Hillingdon got for her at a chemist.'

'Oh, Edward Hillingdon came into it?'

'Oh yes, he was very much attracted. People noticed

it. And Lucky—Miss Greatorex—played them off against each other. Gregory Dyson and Edward Hillingdon. One has to face it, she has always been an attractive woman.'

'Though not as young as she was,' Miss Marple replied.

'Exactly. But she was always very well turned out and made up. Of course not so flamboyant when she was just the poor relation. She always *seemed* very devoted to the invalid. But, well, you see how it was.'

'What was this story about the chemist—how did that get known?'

'Well, it wasn't in Jamestown, I think it was when they were in Martinique. The French, I believe, are more lax than we are in the matter of drugs—This chemist talked to someone, and the story got around—Well, you know how these things happen.'

Miss Marple did. None better.

'He said something about Colonel Hillingdon asking for something and not seeming to know what it was he was asking for. Consulting a piece of paper, you know, on which it was written down. Anyway, as I say, there was *talk*.'

'But I don't see quite why Colonel Hillingdon—' Miss Marple frowned in perplexity.

'I suppose he was just being used as a *cat's-paw*. Anyway, Gregory Dyson married again in an almost indecently short time. Barely a month later, I understand.'

They looked at each other.

'But there was no *real* suspicion?' Miss Marple asked.

'Oh no, it was just—well, *talk*. Of course there may have been absolutely nothing in it.'

'Major Palgrave thought there was.'

'Did he say so to you?'

'I wasn't really listening very closely,' confessed Miss Marple. 'I just wondered if—er—well, if he'd said the same things to you?'

'He did point her out to me one day,' said Miss Prescott.

'Really? He actually pointed her out?'

'Yes. As a matter of fact, I thought at first it was Mrs Hillingdon he was pointing out. He wheezed and chuckled a bit and said, "Look at that woman over there. In my opinion that's a woman who's done murder and got away with it." I was very shocked, of course. I said, "Surely you're joking, Major Palgrave," and he said, "Yes, yes, dear lady, let's call it joking." The Dysons and the Hillingdons were sitting at a table quite near to us, and I was afraid they'd overhear. He chuckled and said "Wouldn't care to go to a drinks party and have a certain person mix me a cocktail. Too much like supper with the Borgias."'

'How *very* interesting,' said Miss Marple. 'Did he mention—a—a photograph?'

'I don't remember . . . Was it some newspaper cutting?'

Miss Marple, about to speak, shut her lips. The sun was momentarily obscured by a shadow. Evelyn Hillingdon paused beside them.

'Good morning,' she said.

'I was wondering where you were,' said Miss Prescott, looking up brightly.

'I've been to Jamestown, shopping.'

'Oh, I see.'

Miss Prescott looked round vaguely and Evelyn Hillingdon said:

'Oh, I didn't take Edward with me. Men hate shopping.'

'Did you find anything of interest?'

'It wasn't that sort of shopping. I just had to go to the chemist.'

With a smile and a slight nod she went on down the beach.

'Such nice people, the Hillingdons,' said Miss Prescott, 'though she's not really very easy to know, is she? I mean, she's always very pleasant and all that, but one never seems to get to know her any better.'

Miss Marple agreed thoughtfully.

'One never knows what she is thinking,' said Miss Prescott.

'Perhaps that is just as well,' said Miss Marple.

'I beg your pardon?'

'Oh nothing really, only that I've always had the feeling that perhaps her thoughts might be rather disconcerting.'

'Oh,' said Miss Prescott, looking puzzled. 'I see what you mean.' She went on with a slight change of subject. 'I believe they have a very charming place in Hampshire, and a boy—or is it two boys—who have just gone—or one of them—to Winchester.'

'Do you know Hampshire well?'

'No. Hardly at all. I believe their house is somewhere near Alton.'

'I see.' Miss Marple paused and then said, 'And where do the Dysons live?'

'California,' said Miss Prescott. 'When they are at home, that is. They are great travellers.'

'One really knows so little about the people one meets when one is travelling,' said Miss Marple. 'I mean—how shall I put it—one only knows, doesn't one, what they choose to tell you about themselves. For instance, you don't *really* know that the Dysons live in California.'

Miss Prescott looked startled.

'I'm sure Mr Dyson mentioned it.'

'Yes. Yes, exactly. That's what I mean. And the same thing perhaps with the Hillingdons. I mean when you say that they live in Hampshire, you're really repeating what *they* told *you*, aren't you?'

Miss Prescott looked slightly alarmed. 'Do you mean that they don't live in Hampshire?' she asked.

'No, no, not for one moment,' said Miss Marple, quickly apologetic. 'I was only using them as an instance as to what one knows or doesn't know about people.' She added, '*I* have told you that I live at St Mary Mead, which is a place, no doubt, of which you have never heard. But you don't, if I may say so, know it of your *own* knowledge, do you?'

Miss Prescott forbore from saying that she really couldn't care less *where* Miss Marple lived. It was somewhere in the country and in the South of England and that is all she knew. 'Oh, I do see what you mean,' she agreed hastily, 'and I know that one can't possibly be too careful when one is abroad.'

'I didn't exactly mean *that*,' said Miss Marple.

There were some odd thoughts going through Miss

Agatha Christie

Marple's mind. Did she really know, she was asking herself, that Canon Prescott and Miss Prescott were really Canon Prescott and Miss Prescott? They said so. There was no evidence to contradict them. It would really be easy, would it not, to put on a dog-collar, to wear the appropriate clothes, to make the appropriate conversation. If there was a motive . . .

Miss Marple was fairly knowledgeable about the clergy in her part of the world, but the Prescotts came from the north. Durham, wasn't it? She had no doubt they were the Prescotts, but still, it came back to the same thing— one believed what people said to one.

Perhaps one ought to be on one's guard against that. Perhaps . . . She shook her head thoughtfully.

CHAPTER 19

Uses of a Shoe

Canon Prescott came back from the water's edge slightly short of breath (playing with children is always exhausting).

Presently he and his sister went back to the hotel, finding the beach a little too hot.

'But,' said Señora de Caspearo scornfully as they walked away—'how can a beach be too hot? It is nonsense that— And look what she wears—her arms and her neck are all covered up. Perhaps it is as well, that. Her skin it is hideous, like a plucked chicken!'

Miss Marple drew a deep breath. Now or never was the time for conversation with Señora de Caspearo. Unfortunately she did not know what to say. There seemed to be no common ground on which they could meet.

'You have children, Señora?' she inquired.

'I have three angels,' said Señora de Caspearo, kissing her fingertips.

Miss Marple was rather uncertain as to whether this meant that Señora de Caspearo's offspring were in Heaven or whether it merely referred to their characters.

One of the gentlemen in attendance made a remark in Spanish and Señora de Caspearo flung back her head appreciatively and laughed loudly and melodiously.

'You understand what he said?' she inquired of Miss Marple.

'I'm afraid not,' said Miss Marple apologetically.

'It is just as well. He is a wicked man.'

A rapid and spirited interchange of Spanish badinage followed.

'It is infamous—infamous,' said Señora de Caspearo, reverting to English with sudden gravity, 'that the police do not let us go from this island. I storm, I scream, I stamp my foot—but all they say is No—No. You know how it will end—we shall all be killed.'

Her bodyguard attempted to reassure her.

'But yes—I tell you it is unlucky here. I knew it from the first—That old Major, the ugly one—he had the Evil Eye—you remember? His eyes they crossed—It is bad, that! I make the Sign of the Horns every time when he looks my way.' She made it in illustration. 'Though since he is cross-eyed I am not always sure when he does look my way—'

'He had a glass eye,' said Miss Marple in an explanatory voice. 'An accident, I understand, when he was quite young. It was not his fault.'

'I tell you he brought bad luck—I say it is the Evil Eye he had.'

Her hand shot out again in the well-known Latin gesture—the first finger and the little finger sticking out, the two middle ones doubled in. 'Anyway,' she said

170

cheerfully, 'he is dead—I do not have to look at him any more. I do not like to look at things that are ugly.'

It was, Miss Marple thought, a somewhat cruel epitaph on Major Palgrave.

Farther down the beach Gregory Dyson had come out of the sea. Lucky had turned herself over on the sand. Evelyn Hillingdon was looking at Lucky, and her expression, for some reason, made Miss Marple shiver.

'Surely I can't be cold—in this hot sun,' she thought.

What was the old phrase—'*A goose walking over your grave*—'

She got up and went slowly back to her bungalow.

On the way she passed Mr Rafiel and Esther Walters coming down the beach. Mr Rafiel winked at her. Miss Marple did not wink back. She looked disapproving.

She went into her bungalow and lay down on her bed. She felt old and tired and worried.

She was quite certain that there was no time to be lost—no time—to—be lost . . . It was getting late . . . The sun was going to set—the sun—one must always look at the sun through smoked glass—Where was that piece of smoked glass that someone had given her? . . .

No, she wouldn't need it after all. A shadow had come over the sun blotting it out. A shadow. Evelyn Hillingdon's shadow—No, not Evelyn Hillingdon—The Shadow (what were the words?) the *Shadow of the Valley of Death*. That was it. She must—what was it? Make the Sign of the Horns—to avert the Evil Eye—Major Palgrave's Evil Eye.

Her eyelids flickered open—she had been asleep. But there *was* a shadow—someone peering in at her window.

Agatha Christie

The shadow moved away—and Miss Marple saw who it was—It was Jackson.

'Impertinence—peering in like that,' she thought—and added parenthetically, 'Just like Jonas Parry.'

The comparison reflected no credit on Jackson.

Then she wondered *why* Jackson had been peering into her bedroom. To see if she was there? Or to note that she was there, but was asleep.

She got up, went into the bathroom and peered cautiously through the window.

Arthur Jackson was standing by the door of the bungalow next door. Mr Rafiel's bungalow. She saw him give a rapid glance round and then slip quickly inside. Interesting, thought Miss Marple. Why did he have to look round in that furtive manner? Nothing in the world could have been more natural than his going into Mr Rafiel's bungalow since he himself had a room at the back of it. He was always going in and out of it on some errand or other. So why that quick, guilty glance round? 'Only one reason,' said Miss Marple answering her own question, 'he wanted to be sure that nobody was observing him enter at this particular moment because of something he was going to do in there.'

Everybody, of course, was on the beach at this moment except those who had gone for expeditions. In about twenty minutes or so, Jackson himself would arrive on the beach in the course of his duties to aid Mr Rafiel to take his sea dip. If he wanted to do anything in the bungalow unobserved, now was a very good time. He had satisfied himself that Miss Marple was asleep on her bed, he had satisfied himself that there was nobody near at hand to observe his movements. Well, she must do her best to do exactly that.

Sitting down on her bed, Miss Marple removed her neat sandal shoes and replaced them with a pair of plimsolls. Then she shook her head, removed the plimsolls, burrowed in her suitcase and took out a pair of shoes the heel on one of which she had recently caught on a hook by the door. It was now in a slightly precarious state and Miss Marple adroitly rendered it even more precarious by attention with a nail file. Then she emerged with due precaution from her door walking in stockinged feet. With all the care of a Big Game Hunter approaching up-wind of a herd of antelope, Miss Marple gently circumnavigated Mr Rafiel's bungalow.

Cautiously she manoeuvred her way around the corner of the house. She put on one of the shoes she was carrying, gave a final wrench to the heel of the other, sank gently to her knees and lay prone under the window. If Jackson heard anything, if he came to the window to look out, an old lady would have had a fall owing to the heel coming off her shoe. But evidently Jackson had heard nothing.

Very, very gently Miss Marple raised her head. The windows of the bungalow were low. Shielding herself slightly with a festoon of creeper she peered inside . . .

Jackson was on his knees before a suitcase. The lid of the suitcase was up and Miss Marple could see that it was a specially fitted affair containing compartments filled with various kinds of papers. Jackson was looking through the papers, occasionally drawing documents out of long envelopes. Miss Marple did not remain at her observation post for long. All she wanted was to know what Jackson was doing. She knew now. Jackson was snooping. Whether he was looking for something in particular, or whether he was just indulging his natural instincts, she had no means of judging. But it confirmed her in her belief that Arthur Jackson and Jonas Parry had strong affinities in other things than facial resemblance.

Her problem was now to withdraw. Very carefully she dropped down again and crept along the flower-bed until she was clear of the window. She returned to her bungalow and carefully put away the shoe and the heel that she had detached from it. She looked at them with affection. A good device which she could use on another day if necessary. She resumed her own sandal shoes, and went thoughtfully down to the beach again.

Choosing a moment when Esther Walters was in the water, Miss Marple moved into the chair Esther had vacated.

Greg and Lucky were laughing and talking with Señora de Caspearo and making a good deal of noise.

Miss Marple spoke very quietly, almost under her breath, without looking at Mr Rafiel.

'Do you know that Jackson snoops?'

'Doesn't surprise me,' said Mr Rafiel. 'Caught him at it, did you?'

'I managed to observe him through a window. He had one of your suitcases open and was looking through your papers.'

'Must have managed to get hold of a key to it.

Resourceful fellow. He'll be disappointed though. Nothing he gets hold of in that way will do him a mite of good.'

'He's coming down now,' said Miss Marple, glancing up towards the hotel.

'Time for that idiotic sea dip of mine.'

He spoke again—very quietly.

'As for you—don't be too enterprising. We don't want to be attending *your* funeral next. Remember your age, and be careful. There's somebody about who isn't too scrupulous, remember.'

CHAPTER 20

Night Alarm

Evening came—The lights came up on the terrace—People dined and talked and laughed, albeit less loudly and merrily than they had a day or two ago—The steel band played.

But the dancing ended early. People yawned—went off to bed—The lights went out—There was darkness and stillness—The Golden Palm Tree slept . . .

'Evelyn. Evelyn!' The whisper came sharp and urgent.

Evelyn Hillingdon stirred and turned on her pillow.

'*Evelyn*. Please wake up.'

Evelyn Hillingdon sat up abruptly. Tim Kendal was standing in the doorway. She stared at him in surprise.

'Evelyn, *please*, could you come? It's—Molly. She's ill. I don't know what's the matter with her. I think she must have taken something.'

Evelyn was quick, decisive.

'All right, Tim. I'll come. You go back to her. I'll be with you in a moment.'

Tim Kendal disappeared. Evelyn slipped out of bed,

threw on a dressing-gown and looked across at the other bed. Her husband, it seemed, had not been awakened. He lay there, his head turned away, breathing quietly. Evelyn hesitated for a moment, then decided not to disturb him. She went out of the door and walked rapidly to the main building and beyond it to the Kendals' bungalow. She caught up with Tim in the doorway.

Molly lay in bed. Her eyes were closed and her breathing was clearly not natural. Evelyn bent over her, rolled up an eyelid, felt her pulse and then looked at the bedside table. There was a glass there which had been used. Beside it was an empty phial of tablets. She picked it up.

'They were her sleeping pills,' said Tim, 'but that bottle was half full yesterday or the day before. I think she must have taken the lot.'

'Go and get Dr Graham,' said Evelyn, 'and on the way knock them up and tell them to make strong coffee. Strong as possible. Hurry.'

Tim dashed off. Just outside the doorway he collided with Edward Hillingdon.

'Oh, sorry, Edward.'

'What's happening here?' demanded Hillingdon. 'What's going on?'

'It's Molly. Evelyn's with her. I must get hold of the doctor. I suppose I ought to have gone to him first but I—I wasn't sure and I thought Evelyn would know. Molly would have hated it if I'd fetched a doctor when it wasn't necessary.'

He went off, running. Edward Hillingdon looked after him for a moment and then he walked into the bedroom.

'What's happening?' he said. 'Is it serious?'

'Oh, there you are, Edward. I wondered if you'd woken up. This silly child has been taking things.'

'Is it bad?'

'One can't tell without knowing how much she's taken. I shouldn't think it was too bad if we get going in time. I've sent for coffee. If we can get some of that down her—'

'But why should she do such a thing? You don't think—' He stopped.

'What don't I think?' said Evelyn.

'You don't think it's because of the inquiry—the police—all that?'

'It's possible, of course. That sort of thing could be very alarming to a nervous type.'

'Molly never used to seem a nervous type.'

'One can't really tell,' said Evelyn. 'It's the most unlikely people sometimes who lose their nerve.'

'Yes, I remember . . .' Again he stopped.

'The truth is,' said Evelyn, 'that one doesn't really know anything about anybody.' She added, 'Not even the people who are nearest to you . . .'

'Isn't that going a little too far, Evelyn—exaggerating too much?'

'I don't think it is. When you think of people, it is in the image you have made of them for yourself.'

'I know you,' said Edward Hillingdon quietly.

'You think you do.'

'No. I'm sure.' He added, 'And you're sure of me.'

Evelyn looked at him then turned back to the bed. She took Molly by the shoulders and shook her.

'We ought to be doing something, but I suppose it's better to wait until Dr Graham comes—Oh, I think I hear them.'

'She'll do now.' Dr Graham stepped back, wiped his forehead with a handkerchief and breathed a sigh of relief.

'You think she'll be all right, sir?' Tim demanded anxiously.

'Yes, yes. We got to her in good time. Anyway, she probably didn't take enough to kill her. A couple of days and she'll be as right as rain but she'll have a rather nasty day or two first.' He picked up the empty bottle. 'Who gave her these things anyway?'

'A doctor in New York. She wasn't sleeping well.'

'Well, well. I know all we medicos hand these things out freely nowadays. Nobody tells young women who can't sleep to count sheep, or get up and eat a biscuit, or write a couple of letters and then go back to bed. Instant remedies, that's what people demand nowadays. Sometimes I think it's a pity we give them to them. You've got to learn to put up with things in life. All very well to stuff a comforter into a baby's mouth to stop it crying. Can't go on doing that all a person's life.' He gave a small chuckle. 'I bet you, if you asked Miss Marple what she does if she can't sleep, she'd tell you she counted sheep going under a gate.' He turned back to the bed where Molly was stirring. Her eyes were open now. She looked at them without interest or recognition. Dr Graham took her hand.

'Well, well, my dear, and what have you been doing to yourself?'

She blinked but did not reply.

'Why did you do it, Molly, why? Tell me why?' Tim took her other hand.

Still her eyes did not move. If they rested on anyone it was on Evelyn Hillingdon. There might have been even a faint question in them but it was hard to tell. Evelyn spoke as though there had been the question.

'Tim came and fetched me,' she said.

Her eyes went to Tim, then shifted to Dr Graham.

'You're going to be all right now,' said Dr Graham, 'but don't do it again.'

'She didn't mean to do it,' said Tim quietly. 'I'm sure she didn't mean to do it. She just wanted a good night's rest. Perhaps the pills didn't work at first and so she took more of them. Is that it, Molly?'

Her head moved very faintly in a negative motion.

'You mean—you took them on purpose?' said Tim.

Molly spoke then. 'Yes,' she said.

'But why, Molly, why?'

The eyelids faltered. 'Afraid.' The word was just heard.

'Afraid? Of what?'

But her eyelids closed down.

'Better let her be,' said Dr Graham. Tim spoke impetuously.

'Afraid of what? The police? Because they've been hounding you, asking you questions? I don't wonder. Anyone might feel frightened. But it's just their way, that's all. Nobody thinks for one moment—' he broke off.

Dr Graham made him a decisive gesture.

'I want to go to sleep,' said Molly.

'The best thing for you,' said Dr Graham.

He moved to the door and the others followed him.

'She'll sleep all right,' said Graham.

'Is there anything I ought to do?' asked Tim. He had the usual, slightly apprehensive attitude of a man in illness.

'I'll stay if you like,' said Evelyn kindly.

'Oh no. No, that's quite all right,' said Tim.

Evelyn went back towards the bed. 'Shall I stay with you, Molly?'

Molly's eyes opened again. She said, 'No,' and then after a pause, 'just Tim.'

Tim came back and sat down by the bed.

'I'm here, Molly,' he said and took her hand. 'Just go to sleep. I won't leave you.'

She sighed faintly and her eyes closed.

The doctor paused outside the bungalow and the Hillingdons stood with him.

'You're sure there's nothing more I can do?' asked Evelyn.

'I don't think so, thank you, Mrs Hillingdon. She'll be better with her husband now. But possibly tomorrow—after all, he's got this hotel to run—I think someone should be with her.'

'D'you think she might—try again?' asked Hillingdon.

Graham rubbed his forehead irritably.

'One never knows in these cases. Actually, it's most unlikely. As you've seen for yourselves, the restorative treatment is extremely unpleasant. But of course one can

181

never be absolutely certain. She may have more of this stuff hidden away somewhere.'

'I should never have thought of suicide in connection with a girl like Molly,' said Hillingdon.

Graham said dryly, 'It's not the people who are always talking of killing themselves, threatening to do so, who do it. They dramatize themselves that way and let off steam.'

'Molly always seemed such a happy girl. I think perhaps'—Evelyn hesitated—'I ought to tell you, Dr Graham.' She told him then about her interview with Molly on the beach the night that Victoria had been killed. Graham's face was very grave when she had finished.

'I'm glad you've told me, Mrs Hillingdon. There are very definite indications there of some kind of deep-rooted trouble. Yes. I'll have a word with her husband in the morning.'

'I want to talk to you seriously, Kendal, about your wife.'

They were sitting in Tim's office. Evelyn Hillingdon had taken his place by Molly's bedside and Lucky had promised to come and, as she expressed it, 'spell her' later. Miss Marple had also offered her services. Poor Tim was torn between his hotel commitments and his wife's condition.

'I can't understand it,' said Tim, 'I can't understand Molly any longer. She's changed. Changed out of all seeming.'

'I understand she's been having bad dreams?'

'Yes. Yes, she complained about them a good deal.'

'For how long?'

'Oh, I don't know. About—oh, I suppose a month—perhaps longer. She—we—thought they were just—well, nightmares, you know.'

'Yes, yes, I quite understand. But what's a much more serious sign is the fact that she seems to have felt afraid of someone. Did she complain about that to you?'

'Well, yes. She said once or twice that—oh, people were following her.'

'Ah! Spying on her?'

'Yes, she did use that term once. She said they were her enemies and they'd followed her here.'

'Did she have enemies, Mr Kendal?'

'No. Of course she didn't.'

'No incident in England, anything you know about before you were married?'

'Oh no, nothing of that kind. She didn't get on with her family very well, that was all. Her mother was rather an eccentric woman, difficult to live with perhaps, but . . .'

'Any signs of mental instability in her family?'

Tim opened his mouth impulsively, then shut it again. He pushed a fountain pen about on the desk in front of him.

The doctor said:

'I must stress the fact that it would be better to tell me, Tim, if that is the case.'

'Well, yes, I believe so. Nothing serious, but I believe there was an aunt or something who was a bit batty. But that's nothing. I mean—well you get that in almost any family.'

'Oh yes, yes, that's quite true. I'm not trying to alarm

Christie

you about that, but it just might show a tendency to—well, to break down or imagine things if any stress arose.'

'I don't really know very much,' said Tim. 'After all, people don't pour out all their family histories to you, do they?'

'No, no. Quite so. She had no former friend—she was not engaged to anyone, anyone who might have threatened her or made jealous threats? That sort of thing?'

'I don't know. I don't think so. Molly *was* engaged to some other man before I came along. Her parents were very against it, I understand, and I think she really stuck to the chap more out of opposition and defiance than anything else.' He gave a sudden half-grin. 'You know what it is when you're young. If people cut up a fuss it makes you much keener on whoever it is.'

Dr Graham smiled too. 'Ah yes, one often sees that. One should never take exception to one's children's objectionable friends. Usually they grow out of them naturally. This man, whoever he was, didn't make threats of any kind against Molly?'

'No, I'm sure he didn't. She would have told me. She said herself she just had a silly adolescent craze on him, mainly because he had such a bad reputation.'

'Yes, yes. Well, that doesn't sound serious. Now there's another thing. Apparently your wife has had what she describes as blackouts. Brief passages of time during which she can't account for her actions. Did you know about that, Tim?'

'No,' said Tim slowly. 'No. I didn't. She never told me. I did notice, you know, now you mention it, that she

184

seemed rather vague sometimes and . . .' He paused, thinking. 'Yes, that explains it. I couldn't understand how she seemed to have forgotten the simplest things, or sometimes not to seem to know what time of day it was. I just thought she was absent-minded, I suppose.'

'What it amounts to, Tim, is just this. I advise you most strongly to take your wife to see a good specialist.'

Tim flushed angrily.

'You mean a mental specialist, I suppose?'

'Now, now, don't be upset by labels. A neurologist, a psychologist, someone who specializes in what the layman calls nervous breakdowns. There's a good man in Kingston. Or there's New York of course. There is something that is causing these nervous terrors of your wife's. Something perhaps for which she hardly knows the reason herself. Get advice about her, Tim. Get advice as soon as possible.'

He clapped his hand on the young man's shoulder and got up.

'There's no immediate worry. Your wife has good friends and we'll all be keeping an eye on her.'

'She won't—you don't think she'll try it again?'

'I think it most unlikely,' said Dr Graham.

'You can't be sure,' said Tim.

'One can never be sure,' said Dr Graham, 'that's one of the first things you learn in my profession.' Again he laid a hand on Tim's shoulder. 'Don't worry too much.'

'That's easy to say,' said Tim as the doctor went out of the door. 'Don't worry, indeed! What does he think I'm made of?'

CHAPTER 21

Jackson on Cosmetics

'You're sure you don't mind, Miss Marple?' said Evelyn Hillingdon.

'No, indeed, my dear,' said Miss Marple. 'I'm only too delighted to be of use in any way. At my age, you know, one feels very useless in the world. Especially when I am in a place like this, just enjoying myself. No duties of any kind. No, I'll be delighted to sit with Molly. You go along on your expedition. Pelican Point, wasn't it?'

'Yes,' said Evelyn. 'Both Edward and I love it. I never get tired of seeing the birds diving down, catching up the fish. Tim's with Molly now. But he's got things to do and he doesn't seem to like her being left alone.'

'He's quite right,' said Miss Marple. 'I wouldn't in his place. One never knows, does one? When anyone has attempted anything of that kind—Well, go along, my dear.'

Evelyn went off to join a little group that was waiting for her. Her husband, the Dysons and three or four other people. Miss Marple checked her knitting requirements, saw that she had all she wanted with her, and walked over towards the Kendals' bungalow.

As she came up on to the loggia she heard Tim's voice through the half-open french window.

'If you'd only tell me *why* you did it, Molly. What made you? Was it anything I did? There must be some reason. If you'd only tell me.'

Miss Marple paused. There was a little pause inside before Molly spoke. Her voice was flat and tired.

'I don't know, Tim, I really don't know. I suppose—something came over me.'

Miss Marple tapped on the window and walked in.

'Oh, there you are, Miss Marple. It is very good of you.'

'Not at all,' said Miss Marple. 'I'm delighted to be of any help. Shall I sit here in this chair? You're looking much better, Molly. I'm so glad.'

'I'm all right,' said Molly. 'Quite all right. Just—oh, just sleepy.'

'I shan't talk,' said Miss Marple. 'You just lie quiet and rest. I'll get on with my knitting.'

Tim Kendal threw her a grateful glance and went out. Miss Marple established herself in her chair.

Molly was lying on her left side. She had a half-stupefied, exhausted look. She said in a voice that was almost a whisper:

'It's very kind of you, Miss Marple. I—I think I'll go to sleep.'

She half turned away on her pillows and closed her eyes. Her breathing grew more regular though it was still far from normal. Long experience of nursing made Miss Marple almost automatically straighten the sheet and tuck it under the mattress on her side of the bed. As she did so her hand encountered something hard and rectangular under the mattress. Rather surprised she took hold of this and pulled it out. It was a book. Miss Marple threw a quick glance at the girl in the bed, but she lay there utterly quiescent. She was evidently asleep. Miss Marple opened the book. It was, she saw, a current work on nervous diseases. It came open naturally at a certain place which gave a description of the onset of persecution mania and various other manifestations of schizophrenia and allied complaints.

It was not a highly technical book, but one that could be easily understood by a layman. Miss Marple's face grew very grave as she read. After a minute or two she closed the book and stayed thinking. Then she bent forward and with care replaced the book where she had found it, under the mattress.

She shook her head in some perplexity. Noiselessly she rose from her chair. She walked the few steps towards the window, then turned her head sharply over her shoulder. Molly's eyes were open but even as Miss Marple turned the eyes shut again. For a minute or two Miss Marple was not quite certain whether she might not have imagined that quick, sharp glance. Was Molly then only pretending to be asleep? That might be natural enough. She might feel that Miss Marple would start talking to her if she showed herself awake. Yes, that could be all it was.

Was she reading into that glance of Molly's a kind of slyness that was somehow innately disagreeable? One doesn't know, Miss Marple thought to herself, one really doesn't know.

She decided that she would try to manage a little talk with Dr Graham as soon as it could be managed. She came back to her chair by the bed. She decided after about five minutes or so that Molly was really asleep. No one could have lain so still, could have breathed so evenly. Miss Marple got up again. She was wearing her plimsolls today. Not perhaps very elegant, but admirably suited to this climate and comfortable and roomy for the feet.

She moved gently round the bedroom, pausing at both of the windows, which gave out in two different directions.

The hotel grounds seemed quiet and deserted. Miss Marple came back and was standing a little uncertainly before regaining her seat, when she thought she heard a faint sound outside. Like the scrape of a shoe on the loggia? She hesitated a moment then she went to the window, pushed it a little farther open, stepped out and turned her head back into the room as she spoke.

'I shall be gone only a very short time, dear,' she said, 'just back to my bungalow, to see where I could possibly have put that pattern. I was so sure I had brought it with me. You'll be quite all right till I come back, won't you?' Then turning her head back, she nodded to herself. 'Asleep, poor child. A good thing.'

She went quietly along the loggia, down the steps and turned sharp right to the path there. Passing along between the screen of some hibiscus bushes an observer might have been curious to see that Miss Marple veered sharply on to the flower-bed, passed round to the back of the bungalow and entered it again through the second door there. This led directly into a small room that Tim sometimes used as an unofficial office and from that into the sitting-room.

Here there were wide curtains semi-drawn to keep the room cool. Miss Marple slipped behind one of them. Then she waited. From the window here she had a good view of anyone who approached Molly's bedroom. It was some few minutes, four or five, before she saw anything.

The neat figure of Jackson in his white uniform went up the steps of the loggia. He paused for a minute at the balcony there, and then appeared to be giving a tiny discreet tap on the door of the window that was ajar. There was no response that Miss Marple could hear. Jackson looked around him, a quick furtive glance, then he slipped inside the open doors. Miss Marple moved to the door which led into the adjoining bathroom. Miss Marple's eyebrows rose in slight surprise. She reflected a minute or two, then walked out into the passageway and into the bathroom by the other door.

Jackson spun round from examining the shelf over the wash-basin. He looked taken aback, which was not surprising.

'Oh,' he said, 'I—I didn't . . .'

'Mr Jackson,' said Miss Marple, in great surprise.

'I thought you'd be here somewhere,' said Jackson.

'Did you want anything?' inquired Miss Marple.

'Actually,' said Jackson, 'I was just looking at Mrs Kendal's brand of face cream.'

Miss Marple appreciated the fact that as Jackson was standing with a jar of face cream in his hand he had been adroit in mentioning the fact at once.

'Nice smell,' he said, wrinkling up his nose. 'Fairly good stuff, as these preparations go. The cheaper brands don't suit every skin. Bring it out in a rash as likely as not. The same thing with face powders sometimes.'

'You seem to be very knowledgeable on the subject,' said Miss Marple.

'Worked in the pharmaceutical line for a bit,' said Jackson. 'One learns to know a good deal about cosmetics there. Put stuff in a fancy jar, package it expensively, and it's astonishing what you could rook women for.'

'Is that what you—?' Miss Marple broke off deliberately.

'Well no, I didn't come in here to talk about cosmetics,' Jackson agreed.

'You've not had much time to think up a lie,' thought Miss Marple to herself. 'Let's see what you'll come out with.'

'Matter of fact,' said Jackson, 'Mrs Walters lent her lipstick to Mrs Kendal the other day. I came in to get it back for her. I tapped on the window and then I saw Mrs Kendal was fast asleep, so I thought it would be quite all right if I just walked across into the bathroom and looked for it.'

'I see,' said Miss Marple. 'And did you find it?'

Jackson shook his head. 'Probably in one of her

handbags,' he said lightly. 'I won't bother. Mrs Walters didn't make a point of it. She only just mentioned it casually.' He went on, surveying the toilet preparations: 'Doesn't have very much, does she? Ah well, doesn't need it at her age. Good natural skin.'

'You must look at women with quite a different eye from ordinary men,' said Miss Marple, smiling pleasantly.

'Yes. I suppose various jobs do alter one's angle.'

'You know a good deal about drugs?'

'Oh yes. Good working acquaintance with them. If you ask me, there are too many of them about nowadays. Too many tranquillizers and pep pills and miracle drugs and all the rest of it. All right if they're given on prescription, but there are too many of them you can get without prescription. Some of them can be dangerous.'

'I suppose so,' said Miss Marple. 'Yes, I suppose so.'

'They have a great effect, you know, on behaviour. A lot of this teenage hysteria you get from time to time. It's not natural causes. The kids've been taking things. Oh, there's nothing new about it. It's been known for ages. Out in the East—not that I've ever been there—all sorts of funny things used to happen. You'd be surprised at some of the things women gave their husbands. In India, for example, in the bad old days, a young wife who married an old husband. Didn't want to get rid of him, I suppose, because she'd have been burnt on the funeral pyre, or if she wasn't burnt she'd have been treated as an outcast by the family. No catch to have been a widow in India in those days. But she could keep an elderly husband under drugs, make him semi-imbecile, give him hallucinations, drive him more or less off his head.' He shook his head. 'Yes, lot of dirty work.'

He went on: 'And witches, you know. There's a lot of interesting things known now about witches. Why did they always confess, why did they admit so readily that they *were* witches, that they had flown on broomsticks to the Witches' Sabbath?'

'Torture,' said Miss Marple.

'Not always,' said Jackson. 'Oh yes, torture accounted for a lot of it, but they came out with some of those confessions almost before torture was mentioned. They didn't so much confess as boast about it. Well, they rubbed themselves with ointment, you know. Anointing they used to call it. Some of the preparations, belladonna, atropine, all that sort of thing; if you rub them on the skin they give you hallucinations of levitation, of flying through the air. They thought it all was genuine, poor devils. And look at the Assassins—medieval people, out in Syria, the Lebanon, somewhere like that. They fed them Indian hemp, gave them hallucinations of Paradise and houris, and endless time. They were told that that was what would happen to them after death, but to attain it they had to go and do a ritual killing. Oh, I'm not putting it in fancy language, but that's what it came to.'

'What it came to,' said Miss Marple, 'is in essence the fact that people are highly credulous.'

'Well yes, I suppose you could put it like that.'

'They believe what they are told,' said Miss Marple. 'Yes indeed, we're all inclined to do that,' she added. Then she said sharply, 'Who told you these stories about India, about the doping of husbands with datura?' And she added sharply, before he could answer, 'Was it Major Palgrave?'

Jackson looked slightly surprised. 'Well—yes, as a matter of fact, it was. He told me a lot of stories like that. Of course most of it must have been before his time, but he seemed to know all about it.'

'Major Palgrave was under the impression that he knew a lot about everything,' said Miss Marple. 'He was often inaccurate in what he told people.' She shook her head thoughtfully. 'Major Palgrave,' she said, 'has a lot to answer for.'

There was a slight sound from the adjoining bedroom. Miss Marple turned her head sharply. She went quickly out of the bathroom into the bedroom. Lucky Dyson was standing just inside the window.

'I—oh! I didn't think you were here, Miss Marple.'

'I just stepped into the bathroom for a moment,' said Miss Marple, with dignity and a faint air of Victorian reserve.

In the bathroom, Jackson grinned broadly. Victorian modesty always amused him.

'I just wondered if you'd like me to sit with Molly for a bit,' said Lucky. She looked over towards the bed. 'She's asleep, isn't she?'

'I think so,' said Miss Marple. 'But it's really quite all right. You go and amuse yourself, my dear. I thought you'd gone on that expedition?'

'I was going,' said Lucky, 'but I had such a filthy headache that at the last moment I cried off. So I thought I might as well make myself useful.'

'That was very nice of you,' said Miss Marple. She reseated herself by the bed and resumed her knitting, 'but I'm *quite* happy here.'

Lucky hesitated for a moment or two and then turned away and went out. Miss Marple waited a moment then tiptoed back into the bathroom, but Jackson had departed, no doubt through the other door. Miss Marple picked up the jar of face cream he had been holding, and slipped it into her pocket.

CHAPTER 22

A Man in Her Life?

Getting a little chat in a natural manner with Dr Graham was not so easy as Miss Marple had hoped. She was particularly anxious not to approach him directly since she did not want to lend undue importance to the questions that she was going to ask him.

Tim was back, looking after Molly, and Miss Marple had arranged that she should relieve him there during the time that dinner was served and he was needed in the dining-room. He had assured her that Mrs Dyson was quite willing to take that on, or even Mrs Hillingdon, but Miss Marple said firmly that they were both young women who liked enjoying themselves and that she herself preferred a light meal early and so that would suit everybody. Tim once again thanked her warmly. Hovering rather uncertainly round the hotel and on the pathway which connected with various bungalows, among them Dr Graham's, Miss Marple tried to plan what she was going to do next.

She had a lot of confused and contradictory ideas in

her head and if there was one thing that Miss Marple did not like, it was to have confused and contradictory ideas. This whole business had started out clearly enough. Major Palgrave with his regrettable capacity for telling stories, his indiscretion that had obviously been overheard and the corollary, his death within twenty-four hours. Nothing difficult about *that*, thought Miss Marple.

But afterwards, she was forced to admit, there was nothing *but* difficulty. Everything pointed in too many different directions at once. Once admit that you didn't believe a word that anybody had said to you, that nobody could be trusted, and that many of the persons with whom she had conversed here had regrettable resemblances to certain persons at St Mary Mead, and where did that lead you?

Her mind was increasingly focused on the victim. Someone was going to be killed and she had the increasing feeling that she ought to know quite well who that someone was. There had been *something*. Something she had heard? Noticed? Seen?

Something someone had told her that had a bearing on the case. Joan Prescott? Joan Prescott had said a lot of things about a lot of people. Scandal? Gossip? What exactly *had* Joan Prescott said?

Gregory Dyson, Lucky—Miss Marple's mind hovered over Lucky. Lucky, she was convinced with a certainty born of her natural suspicions, had been actively concerned in the death of Gregory Dyson's first wife. Everything pointed to it. Could it be that the predestined victim over whom she was worrying was Gregory Dyson? That Lucky intended to try her luck again with another husband, and for that reason wanted not only freedom but the handsome inheritance that she would get as Gregory Dyson's widow?

'But really,' said Miss Marple to herself, 'this is all pure conjecture. I'm being stupid. I know I'm being stupid. The truth must be quite plain, if one could just clear away the litter. Too much litter, that's what's the matter.'

'Talking to yourself?' said Mr Rafiel.

Miss Marple jumped. She had not noticed his approach. Esther Walters was supporting him and he was coming slowly down from his bungalow to the terrace.

'I really didn't notice you, Mr Rafiel.'

'Your lips were moving. What's become of all this urgency of yours?'

'It's still urgent,' said Miss Marple, 'only I can't just see what must be perfectly plain—'

'I'm glad it's as simple as that—Well, if you want any help, count on me.'

He turned his head as Jackson approached them along the path.

'So there you are, Jackson. Where the devil have you been? Never about when I want you.'

'Sorry, Mr Rafiel.'

Dexterously he slipped his shoulder under Mr Rafiel's. 'Down to the terrace, sir?'

'You can take me to the bar,' said Mr Rafiel. 'All right, Esther, you can go now and change into your evening togs. Meet me on the terrace in half an hour.'

He and Jackson went off together. Mrs Walters

dropped into the chair by Miss Marple. She rubbed her arm gently.

'He *seems* a very light weight,' she observed, 'but at the moment my arm feels quite numb. I haven't seen you this afternoon at all, Miss Marple.'

'No, I've been sitting with Molly Kendal,' Miss Marple explained. 'She seems really very much better.'

'If you ask me there was never very much wrong with her,' said Esther Walters.

Miss Marple raised her eyebrows. Esther Walters's tone had been decidedly dry.

'You mean—you think her suicide attempt . . .'

'I don't think there *was* any suicide attempt,' said Esther Walters. 'I don't believe for a moment she took a real overdose and I think Dr Graham knows that perfectly well.'

'Now you interest me very much,' said Miss Marple. 'I wonder why you say that?'

'Because I'm almost certain that it's the case. Oh, it's a thing that happens very often. It's a way, I suppose, of calling attention to oneself,' went on Esther Walters.

'"You'll be sorry when I'm dead"?' quoted Miss Marple.

'That sort of thing,' agreed Esther Walters, 'though I don't think that was the motive in this particular instance. That's the sort of thing you feel like when your husband's playing you up and you're terribly fond of him.'

'You don't think Molly Kendal is fond of her husband?'

'Well,' said Esther Walters, 'do you?'

Miss Marple considered. 'I have,' she said, 'more or less assumed it.' She paused a moment before adding, 'Perhaps wrongly.'

Esther was smiling her rather wry smile.

'I've heard a little about her, you know. About the whole business.'

'From Miss Prescott?'

'Oh,' said Esther, 'from one or two people. There's a man in the case. Someone she was keen on. Her people were dead against him.'

'Yes,' said Miss Marple, 'I did hear that.'

'And then she married Tim. Perhaps she was fond of him in a way. But the other man didn't give up. I've wondered once or twice if he didn't actually follow her out here.'

'Indeed. But—who?'

'I've no idea who,' said Esther, 'and I should imagine that they've been very careful.'

'You think she cares for this other man?'

Esther shrugged her shoulders. 'I dare say he's a bad lot,' she said, 'but that's very often the kind who knows how to get under a woman's skin and stay there.'

'You never heard what kind of a man—what he did— anything like that?'

Esther shook her head. 'No. People hazard guesses, but you can't go by that type of thing. He may have been a married man. That may have been why her people disliked it, or he may have been a real bad lot. Perhaps he drank. Perhaps he tangled with the law—I don't know. But she cares for him still. That I know positively.'

'You've seen something, heard something?' Miss Marple hazarded.

'I know what I'm talking about,' said Esther. Her voice was harsh and unfriendly.

'These murders—' began Miss Marple.

'Can't you forget murders?' said Esther. 'You've got Mr Rafiel now all tangled up in them. Can't you just—let them be? You'll never find out any more, I'm sure of that.'

Miss Marple looked at her.

'You think you know, don't you?' she said.

'I think I do, yes. I'm fairly sure.'

'Then oughtn't you to tell what you know—do something about it?'

'Why should I? What good would it do? I couldn't prove anything. What would happen anyway? People get let off nowadays so easily. They call it diminished responsibility and things like that. A few years in prison and you're out again, as right as rain.'

'Supposing, because you don't tell what you know, somebody else gets killed—another victim?'

Esther shook her head with confidence. 'That won't happen,' she said.

'You can't be sure of it.'

'I am sure. And in any case I don't see who—' She frowned. 'Anyway,' she added, almost inconsequently, 'perhaps it *is*—diminished responsibility. Perhaps you can't help it—not if you are really mentally unbalanced. Oh, I don't know. By far the best thing would be if she went off with whoever it is, then we could all forget about things.'

She glanced at her watch, gave an exclamation of dismay and got up.

'I must go and change.'

Miss Marple sat looking after her. Pronouns, she thought, were always puzzling and women like Esther

Walters were particularly prone to strew them about haphazard. Was Esther Walters for some reason convinced that a *woman* had been responsible for the deaths of Major Palgrave and Victoria? It sounded like it. Miss Marple considered.

'Ah, Miss Marple, sitting here all alone—and not even knitting?'

It was Dr Graham for whom she had sought so long and so unsuccessfully. And here he was prepared of his own accord to sit down for a few minutes' chat. He wouldn't stay long, Miss Marple thought, because he too was bent on changing for dinner, and he usually dined fairly early. She explained that she had been sitting by Molly Kendal's bedside that afternoon.

'One can hardly believe she has made such a good recovery so quickly,' she said.

'Oh well,' said Dr Graham, 'it's not very surprising. She didn't take a very heavy overdose, you know.'

'Oh, I understood she'd taken quite a half-bottle full of tablets.'

Dr Graham was smiling indulgently.

'No,' he said, 'I don't think she took that amount. I dare say she meant to take them, then probably at the last moment she threw half of them away. People, even when they think they want to commit suicide, often don't *really* want to do it. They manage not to take a full overdose. It's not always deliberate deceit, it's just the subconscious looking after itself.'

'Or, I suppose it might be deliberate. I mean, wanting it to appear that . . .' Miss Marple paused.

'It's possible,' said Dr Graham.

'If she and Tim had had a row, for instance?'

'They don't have rows, you know. They seem very fond of each other. Still, I suppose it can always happen once. No, I don't think there's very much wrong with her now. She could really get up and go about as usual. Still, it's safer to keep her where she is for a day or two—'

He got up, nodded cheerfully and went off towards the hotel. Miss Marple sat where she was a little while longer.

Various thoughts passed through her mind—The book under Molly's mattress—The way Molly had feigned sleep—

Things Joan Prescott and, later, Esther Walters, had said . . .

And then she went back to the beginning of it all—to Major Palgrave—

Something struggled in her mind. Something about Major Palgrave—

Something that if she could only remember—

CHAPTER 23

The Last Day

'*And the evening and the morning were the last day,*' said Miss Marple to herself.

Then, slightly confused, she sat upright again in her chair. She had dozed off, an incredible thing to do because the steel band was playing and anyone who could doze off during the steel band—Well, it showed, thought Miss Marple, that she was getting used to this place! What was it she had been saying? Some quotation that she'd got wrong. Last day? *First* day. That's what it ought to be. This wasn't the first day. Presumably it wasn't the last day either.

She sat upright again. The fact was that she was extremely tired. All this anxiety, this feeling of having been shamefully inadequate in some way . . . She remembered unpleasantly once more that queer sly look that Molly had given her from under her half-closed eyelids. What had been going on in that girl's head? How different, thought Miss Marple, everything had seemed at first. Tim Kendal and Molly, such a natural happy young couple.

The Hillingdons so pleasant, so well-bred, such what is called 'nice' people. The gay hearty extrovert, Greg Dyson, and the gay strident Lucky, talking nineteen to the dozen, pleased with herself and the world . . . A quartet of people getting on so well together. Canon Prescott, that genial kindly man. Joan Prescott, an acid streak in her, but a very nice woman, and nice women had to have their gossipy distractions. They have to know what is going on, to know when two and two make four, and when it is possible to stretch them to five! There was no harm in such women. Their tongues wagged but they were kind if you were in misfortune. Mr Rafiel, a personality, a man of character, a man that you would never by any chance forget. But Miss Marple thought she knew something else about Mr Rafiel.

The doctors had often given him up, so he had said, but this time, she thought, they had been more certain in their pronouncements. Mr Rafiel knew that his days were numbered.

Knowing this with certainty, was there any action he might have been likely to take?

Miss Marple considered the question.

It might, she thought, be important.

What was it exactly he had said, his voice a little too loud, a little too sure? Miss Marple was very skilful in tones of voice. She had done so much listening in her life.

Mr Rafiel had been telling her something that wasn't true.

Miss Marple looked round her. The night air, the soft fragrance of flowers, the tables with their little lights, the women with their pretty dresses, Evelyn in a dark indigo and white print, Lucky in a white sheath, her golden hair shining. Everybody seemed gay and full of life tonight. Even Tim Kendal was smiling. He passed her table and said:

'Can't thank you enough for all you've done. Molly's practically herself again. The doc says she can get up tomorrow.'

Miss Marple smiled at him and said that that was good hearing. She found it, however, quite an effort to smile. Decidedly, she was tired . . .

She got up and walked slowly back to her bungalow. She would have liked to go on thinking, puzzling, trying to remember, trying to assemble various facts and words and glances. But she wasn't able to do it. The tired mind rebelled. It said 'Sleep! You've got to go to sleep!'

Miss Marple undressed, got into bed, read a few verses of the Thomas à Kempis which she kept by her bed, then she turned out the light. In the darkness she sent up a prayer. One couldn't do everything oneself. One had to have help. 'Nothing will happen tonight,' she murmured hopefully.

Miss Marple woke suddenly and sat up in bed. Her heart was beating. She switched on the light and looked at the little clock by her bedside. Two a.m. Two a.m. and outside activity of some kind was going on. She got up, put on her dressing-gown and slippers, and a woollen scarf round her head and went out to reconnoitre. There were people moving about with torches. Among them she saw Canon Prescott and went to him.

'What's happening?'

'Oh, Miss Marple? It's Mrs Kendal. Her husband woke up, found she'd slipped out of bed and gone out. We're looking for her.'

He hurried on. Miss Marple walked more slowly after him. Where had Molly gone? Why? Had she planned this deliberately, planned to slip away as soon as the guard on her was relaxed, and while her husband was deep in sleep? Miss Marple thought it was probable. But why? What was the reason? Was there, as Esther Walters had so strongly hinted, some other man? If so, who could that man be? Or was there some more sinister reason?

Miss Marple walked on, looking around her, peering under bushes. Then suddenly she heard a faint call:

'Here . . . This way . . .'

The cry had come from some little distance beyond the hotel grounds. It must be, thought Miss Marple, near the creek of water that ran down to the sea. She went in that direction as briskly as she could.

There were not really so many searchers as it had seemed to her at first. Most people must still be asleep in their bungalows. She saw a place on the creek bank where there were people standing. Someone pushed past her, almost knocking her down, running in that direction. It was Tim Kendal. A minute or two later she heard his voice cry out:

'Molly! My God, Molly!'

It was a minute or two before Miss Marple was able

to join the little group. It consisted of one of the Cuban waiters, Evelyn Hillingdon, and two of the native girls. They had parted to let Tim through. Miss Marple arrived as he was bending over to look.

'Molly . . .' He slowly dropped on to his knees. Miss Marple saw the girl's body clearly, lying there in the creek, her face below the level of the water, her golden hair spread over the pale green embroidered shawl that covered her shoulders. With the leaves and rushes of the creek, it seemed almost like a scene from *Hamlet* with Molly as the dead Ophelia . . .

As Tim stretched out a hand to touch her, the quiet, common-sense Miss Marple took charge and spoke sharply and authoritatively.

'Don't move her, Mr Kendal,' she said. 'She mustn't be moved.'

Tim turned a dazed face up to her.

'But—I must—it's Molly. I must . . .'

Evelyn Hillingdon touched his shoulder.

'She's dead, Tim. I didn't move her, but I did feel her pulse.'

'Dead?' said Tim unbelievingly. 'Dead? You mean she's—*drowned* herself?'

'I'm afraid so. It looks like it.'

'But *why*?' A great cry burst from the young man. '*Why*? She was so happy this morning. Talking about what we'd do tomorrow. Why should this terrible death wish come over her again? Why should she steal away as she did—rush out into the night, come down here and drown herself? What despair did she have—what misery— why couldn't she *tell* me anything?'

208

'I don't know, my dear,' said Evelyn gently. 'I don't know.'

Miss Marple said:

'Somebody had better get Dr Graham. And someone will have to telephone the police.'

'The police?' Tim uttered a bitter laugh. 'What good will they be?'

'The police have to be notified in a case of suicide,' said Miss Marple.

Tim rose slowly to his feet.

'I'll get Graham,' he said heavily. 'Perhaps—even now— he could—do something.'

He stumbled away in the direction of the hotel.

Evelyn Hillingdon and Miss Marple stood side by side looking down at the dead girl.

Evelyn shook her head. 'It's too late. She's quite cold. She must have been dead at least an hour—perhaps more. What a tragedy it all is. Those two always seemed so happy. I suppose she was always unbalanced.'

'No,' said Miss Marple. 'I don't think she was unbalanced.'

Evelyn looked at her curiously. 'What do you mean?'

The moon had been behind a cloud, but now it came out into the open. It shone with a luminous silvery brightness on Molly's outspread hair . . .

Miss Marple gave a sudden ejaculation. She bent down, peering, then stretched out her hand and touched the golden head. She spoke to Evelyn Hillingdon, and her voice sounded quite different.

'I think,' she said, 'that we had better make sure.'

Evelyn Hillingdon stared at her in astonishment.

'But you yourself told Tim we mustn't touch anything?'

'I know. But the moon wasn't out. I hadn't seen—'

Her finger pointed. Then, very gently, she touched the blonde hair and parted it so that the roots were exposed . . .

Evelyn gave a sharp ejaculation.

'*Lucky!*'

And then after a moment she repeated:

'Not Molly . . . Lucky.'

Miss Marple nodded. 'Their hair was of much the same colour—but hers, of course, was dark at the roots because it was dyed.'

'But she's wearing Molly's shawl?'

'She admired it. I heard her say she was going to get one like it. Evidently she did.'

'So that's why we were—deceived . . .'

Evelyn broke off as she met Miss Marple's eyes watching her.

'Someone,' said Miss Marple, 'will have to tell her husband.'

There was a moment's pause, then Evelyn said:

'All right. I'll do it.'

She turned and walked away through the palm trees.

Miss Marple remained for a moment motionless, then she turned her head very slightly, and said:

'Yes, Colonel Hillingdon?'

Edward Hillingdon came from the trees behind her to stand by her side.

'You knew I was there?'

'You cast a shadow,' said Miss Marple.

They stood a moment in silence.

He said, more as though he were speaking to himself: 'So, in the end, she played her luck too far . . .'

'You are, I think, glad that she is dead?'

'And that shocks you? Well, I will not deny it. I am glad she is dead.'

'Death is often a solution to problems.'

Edward Hillingdon turned his head slowly. Miss Marple met his eyes calmly and steadfastly.

'If you think—' he took a sharp step towards her.

There was a sudden menace in his tone.

Miss Marple said quietly:

'Your wife will be back with Mr Dyson in a moment. Or Mr Kendal will be here with Dr Graham.'

Edward Hillingdon relaxed. He turned back to look down at the dead woman.

Miss Marple slipped away quietly. Presently her pace quickened.

Just before reaching her own bungalow, she paused. It was here that she had sat that day talking to Major Palgrave. It was here that he had fumbled in his wallet looking for the snapshot of a murderer . . .

She remembered how he had looked up, and how his face had gone purple and red . . . 'So ugly,' as Señora de Caspearo had said. 'He has the Evil Eye.'

The Evil Eye . . . Eye . . . *Eye* . . .

CHAPTER 24

Nemesis

Whatever the alarms and excursions of the night, Mr Rafiel had not heard them.

He was fast asleep in bed, a faint thin snore coming from his nostrils, when he was taken by the shoulders and shaken violently.

'Eh—what—what the devil's this?'

'It's me,' said Miss Marple, for once ungrammatical, 'though I should put it a little more strongly than that. The Greeks, I believe, had a word for it. Nemesis, if I am not wrong.'

Mr Rafiel raised himself on his pillows as far as he could. He stared at her. Miss Marple, standing there in the moonlight, her head encased in a fluffy scarf of pale pink wool, looked as unlike a figure of Nemesis as it was possible to imagine.

'So you're Nemesis, are you?' said Mr Rafiel after a momentary pause.

'I hope to be—with your help.'

'Do you mind telling me quite plainly what you're talking about like this in the middle of the night?'

'I think we may have to act quickly. Very quickly. I have been foolish. Extremely foolish. I ought to have known from the very beginning what all this was about. It was so simple.'

'What was simple, and what are you talking about?'

'You slept through a good deal,' said Miss Marple. 'A body was found. We thought at first it was the body of Molly Kendal. It wasn't, it was Lucky Dyson. Drowned in the creek.'

'Lucky, eh?' said Mr Rafiel. 'And drowned? In the creek. Did she drown herself or did somebody drown her?'

'Somebody drowned her,' said Miss Marple.

'I see. At least I think I see. That's what you mean by saying it's so simple, is it? Greg Dyson was always the first possibility, and he's the right one. Is that it? Is that what you're thinking? And what you're afraid of is that he may get away with it.'

Miss Marple took a deep breath.

'Mr Rafiel, will you trust me? We have got to stop a murder being committed.'

'I thought you said it *had* been committed.'

'That murder was committed in error. Another murder may be committed any moment now. There's no time to lose. We must prevent it happening. We must go at once.'

'It's all very well to talk like that,' said Mr Rafiel. '*We*, you say? What do you think *I* can do about it? I can't even walk without help. How can you and I set about preventing a murder? You're about a hundred and I'm a broken-up old crock.'

'I was thinking of Jackson,' said Miss Marple. 'Jackson will do what you tell him, won't he?'

'He will indeed,' said Mr Rafiel, 'especially if I add that I'll make it worth his while. Is that what you want?'

'Yes. Tell him to come with me and tell him to obey any orders I give him.'

Mr Rafiel looked at her for about six seconds. Then he said:

'Done. I expect I'm taking the biggest risk of my life. Well, it won't be the first one.' He raised his voice. 'Jackson.' At the same time he picked up the electric bell that lay beside his hand and pressed the button.

Hardly thirty seconds passed before Jackson appeared through the connecting door to the adjoining room.

'You called and rang, sir? Anything wrong?' He broke off, staring at Miss Marple.

'Now, Jackson, do as I tell you. You will go with this lady, Miss Marple. You'll go where she takes you and you'll do exactly as she says. You'll obey every order she gives you. Is that understood?'

'I—'

'*Is that understood*?'

'Yes, sir.'

'And for doing that,' said Mr Rafiel, 'you won't be the loser. I'll make it worth your while.'

'Thank you, sir.'

'Come along, Mr Jackson,' said Miss Marple. She spoke over her shoulder to Mr Rafiel. 'We'll tell Mrs Walters to come to you on your way. Get her to get you out of bed and bring you along.'

'Bring me along where?'

'To the Kendals' bungalow,' said Miss Marple. 'I think Molly will be coming back there.'

Molly came up the path from the sea. Her eyes stared fixedly ahead of her. Occasionally, under her breath, she gave a little whimper . . .

She went up the steps of the loggia, paused a moment, then pushed open the window and walked into the bedroom. The lights were on, but the room itself was empty. Molly went across to the bed and sat down. She sat for some minutes, now and again passing her hand over her forehead and frowning.

Then, after a quick surreptitious glance round, she slipped her hand under the mattress and brought out the book that was hidden there. She bent over it, turning the pages to find what she wanted.

Then she raised her head as a sound of running footsteps came from outside. With a quick guilty movement she pushed the book behind her back.

Tim Kendal, panting and out of breath, came in, and uttered a great sigh of relief at the sight of her.

'Thank God. Where have you been, Molly? I've been searching everywhere for you.'

'I went to the creek.'

'You went—' he stopped.

'Yes. I went to the creek. But I couldn't wait there. I couldn't. There was someone in the water—and she was dead.'

'You mean—Do you know I thought it was *you*? I've only just found out it was Lucky.'

'I didn't kill her. Really, Tim, I didn't kill her. I'm sure I didn't. I mean—I'd remember if I did, wouldn't I?'

Tim sank slowly down on the end of the bed.

'You didn't—Are you sure that—? No. No, of course you didn't!' He fairly shouted the words. 'Don't start thinking like that, Molly. Lucky drowned herself. Of course she drowned herself. Hillingdon was through with her. She went and lay down with her face in the water—'

'Lucky wouldn't do that. She'd never do that. But *I* didn't kill her. I swear I didn't.'

'Darling, of course you didn't!' He put his arms round her but she pulled herself away.

'I hate this place. It ought to be all sunlight. It seemed to be all sunlight. But it isn't. Instead there's a shadow—a big black shadow . . . And I'm in it—and I can't get out—'

Her voice had risen to a shout.

'Hush, Molly. For God's sake, hush!' He went into the bathroom, came back with a glass.

'Look. Drink this. It'll steady you.'

'I—I can't drink anything. My teeth are chattering so.'

'Yes you can, darling. Sit down. Here, on the bed.' He put his arm round her. He approached the glass to her lips. 'There you are now. Drink it.'

A voice spoke from the window.

'Jackson,' said Miss Marple clearly. 'Go over. Take that glass from him and hold it tightly. Be careful. He's strong and he may be pretty desperate.'

There were certain points about Jackson. He was a

man with a great love for money, and money had been promised him by his employer, that employer being a man of stature and authority. He was also a man of extreme muscular development heightened by his training. His not to reason why, his but to do.

Swift as a flash he had crossed the room. His hand went over the glass that Tim was holding to Molly's lips, his other arm had fastened round Tim. A quick flick of the wrist and he had the glass. Tim turned on him wildly, but Jackson held him firmly.

'What the devil—let go of me. Let go of me. Have you gone mad? What are you doing?'

Tim struggled violently.

'Hold him, Jackson,' said Miss Marple.

'What's going on? What's the matter here?'

Supported by Esther Walters, Mr Rafiel came through the window.

'You ask what's the matter?' shouted Tim. 'Your man's gone mad, stark, staring mad, that's what's the matter. Tell him to let go of me.'

'No,' said Miss Marple.

Mr Rafiel turned to her.

'Speak up, Nemesis,' he said. 'We've got to have chapter and verse of some kind.'

'I've been stupid and a fool,' said Miss Marple, 'but I'm not being a fool now. When the contents of that glass that he was trying to make his wife drink have been analysed, I'll wager—yes, I'll wager my immortal soul that you'll find it's got a lethal dose of narcotic in it. It's the same pattern, you see, the same pattern as in Major

Palgrave's story. A wife in a depressed state, and she tries to do away with herself, husband saves her in time. Then the second time she succeeds. Yes, it's the right pattern. Major Palgrave told me the story and he took out a snapshot and then he looked up and saw—'

'Over your right shoulder—' continued Mr Rafiel.

'No,' said Miss Marple, shaking her head. '*He didn't see anything over my right shoulder.*'

'What are you talking about? You told me . . .'

'I told you wrong. I was completely wrong. I was stupid beyond belief. Major Palgrave *appeared* to me to be looking over my right shoulder, glaring, in fact, at something—But he couldn't have *seen* anything, because he was looking through his left eye and his left eye was his glass eye.'

'I remember—he *had* a glass eye,' said Mr Rafiel. 'I'd forgotten—or I took it for granted. You mean he couldn't see anything?'

'Of course he could *see*,' said Miss Marple. 'He could *see* all right, but he could only see with one eye. The eye he *could* see with was his *right* eye. And so, you see, he must have been looking at something or someone not to the right of me but to the *left* of me.'

'Was there anyone on the left of you?'

'Yes,' said Miss Marple. 'Tim Kendal and his wife were sitting not far off. Sitting at a table just by a big hibiscus bush. They were doing accounts there. So you see the Major looked up. His glass left eye was glaring over my shoulder, but what he *saw* with his other eye was a man sitting by a hibiscus bush and the face was the same, only rather older, as the face in the snapshot. Also by a hibiscus bush. Tim Kendal had heard the story the Major had been telling and he saw that the Major had recognized him. So, of course, he had to kill him. Later, he had to kill the girl, Victoria, because she'd seen him putting a bottle of tablets in the Major's room. She didn't think anything of it at first because of course it was quite natural on various occasions for Tim Kendal to go into the guests' bungalows. He might have just been returning something to it that had been left on a restaurant table. But she thought about it and then she asked him questions and so he had to get rid of her. But this is the real murder, the murder he's been planning all along. He's a wife-killer, you see.'

'What damned nonsense, what—' Tim Kendal shouted.

There was a sudden cry, a wild angry cry. Esther Walters detached herself from Mr Rafiel, almost flinging him down, and rushed across the room. She pulled vainly at Jackson.

'Let go of him—let go of him. It's not true. Not a word of it's true. Tim—Tim darling, it's not true. You could never kill anyone, I know you couldn't. I know you wouldn't. It's that horrible girl you married. She's been telling lies about you. They're not true. None of them are true. I believe in you. I love you and trust in you. I'll never believe a word anyone says. I'll—'

Then Tim Kendal lost control of himself.

'For God's sake, you damned bitch,' he said, 'shut up, can't you? D'you want to get me hanged? Shut up, I tell you. Shut that big, ugly mouth of yours.'

'Poor silly creature,' said Mr Rafiel softly. 'So that's what's been going on, is it?'

219

CHAPTER 25

Miss Marple Uses Her Imagination

'So that's what had been going on?' said Mr Rafiel. He and Miss Marple were sitting together in a confidential manner.

'She'd been having an affair with Tim Kendal, had she?'

'Hardly an affair, I imagine,' said Miss Marple, primly. 'It was, I think, a romantic attachment with the prospect of marriage in the future.'

'What—after his wife was dead?'

'I don't think poor Esther Walters knew that Molly was going to die,' said Miss Marple. 'I just think she believed the story Tim Kendal told her about Molly having been in love with another man, and the man having followed her here, and I think she counted on Tim's getting a divorce. I think it was all quite proper and respectable. But she was very much in love with him.'

'Well, that's easily understood. He was an attractive chap. But what made *him* go for her—d'you know that too?'

'*You* know, don't you?' said Miss Marple.

'I dare say I've got a pretty fair idea, but I don't know how you should know about it. As far as that goes, I don't see how Tim Kendal could know about it.'

'Well, I really think I could explain all that with a little imagination, though it would be simpler if you told me.'

'I'm not going to tell you,' said Mr Rafiel. 'You tell me, since you're being so clever.'

'Well, it seems to me possible,' said Miss Marple, 'that as I have already hinted to you, your man Jackson was in the habit of taking a good snoop through your various papers from time to time.'

'Perfectly possible,' said Mr Rafiel, 'but I shouldn't have said there was anything there that could do him much good. I took care of that.'

'I imagine,' said Miss Marple, 'he read your will.'

'Oh I see. Yes, yes, I did have a copy of my will along.'

'You told me,' said Miss Marple, 'you told me—(as Humpty Dumpty said—very loud and clear) that you had *not* left anything to Esther Walters in your will. You had impressed that fact upon her, and also upon Jackson. It was true in Jackson's case, I should imagine. You have not left *him* anything, but you *had* left Esther Walters money, though you weren't going to let her have any inkling of the fact. Isn't that right?'

'Yes, it's quite right, but I don't know how *you* knew.'

'Well, it's the way you insisted on the point,' said Miss Marple. 'I have a certain experience of the way people tell lies.'

'I give in,' said Mr Rafiel. 'All right. I left Esther £50,000. It would come as a nice surprise to her when I died. I suppose that, knowing this, Tim Kendal decided to exterminate his present wife with a nice dose of something or other and marry £50,000 and Esther Walters. Possibly to dispose of her also in good time. But how did *he* know she was going to have £50,000?'

'Jackson told him, of course,' said Miss Marple. 'They were very friendly, those two. Tim Kendal was nice to Jackson and, quite, I should imagine, without ulterior motive. But amongst the bits of gossip that Jackson let slip I think Jackson told him that unbeknownst to herself, Esther Walters was going to inherit a fat lot of money, and he may have said that he himself hoped to induce Esther Walters to marry him though he hadn't had much success so far in taking her fancy. Yes, I think that's how it happened.'

'The things you imagine always seem perfectly plausible,' said Mr Rafiel.

'But I was stupid,' said Miss Marple, 'very stupid. Everything fitted in really, you see. Tim Kendal was a very clever man as well as being a very wicked one. He was particularly good at putting about rumours. Half the things I've been told here came from him originally, I imagine. There were stories going around about Molly wanting to marry an undesirable young man, but I rather fancy that the undesirable young man was actually Tim Kendal himself, though that wasn't the name he was using then. Her people had heard something, perhaps that his background was fishy. So he put on a high indignation act, refused to be taken by Molly to be "shown off" to her people and then he brewed up a little scheme with her which they both thought great fun. She pretended to sulk and pine for him. Then a Mr Tim Kendal turned up, primed with the names of various old friends of Molly's people, and they welcomed him with open arms as being the sort of young man who would put the former delinquent one out of Molly's head. I am afraid Molly and he must have laughed over it a good deal. Anyway, he married her, and with her money he bought out the people who ran this place and they came out here. I should imagine that he ran through her money at a pretty fair rate. Then he came across Esther Walters and he saw a nice prospect of more money.'

'Why didn't he bump me off?' said Mr Rafiel.

Miss Marple coughed.

'I expect he wanted to be fairly sure of Mrs Walters first. Besides—I mean . . .' She stopped, a little confused.

'Besides, he realized he wouldn't have to wait long,' said Mr Rafiel, 'and it would clearly be better for me to die a natural death. Being so rich. Deaths of millionaires are scrutinized rather carefully, aren't they, unlike mere wives?'

'Yes, you're quite right. Such a lot of lies as he told,' said Miss Marple. 'Look at the lies he got Molly herself to believe—putting that book on mental disorders in her way. Giving her drugs which would give her dreams and hallucinations. You know, your Jackson was rather clever over that. I think he recognized certain of Molly's symptoms as being the result of drugs. And he came into the bungalow that day to potter about a bit in the bathroom. That face cream he examined. He might have got some

Agatha Christie

idea from the old tales of witches rubbing themselves with ointments that had belladonna in them. Belladonna in face cream could have produced just that result. Molly would have blackouts. Times she couldn't account for, dreams of flying through the air. No wonder she got frightened about herself. She had all the signs of mental illness, Jackson was on the right track. Maybe he got the idea from Major Palgrave's stories about the use of datura by Indian women on their husbands.'

'Major Palgrave!' said Mr Rafiel. 'Really, that man!'

'He brought about his own murder,' said Miss Marple, 'and that poor girl Victoria's murder, and he nearly brought about Molly's murder. But he recognized a murderer all right.'

'What made you suddenly remember about his glass eye?' asked Mr Rafiel curiously.

'Something that Señora de Caspearo said. She talked some nonsense about his being ugly, and having the Evil Eye; and I said it was only a glass eye, and he couldn't help that, poor man, and she said his eyes looked different ways, they were cross-eyes—which, of course, they were. And she said it brought bad luck. I knew—I *knew* that I had heard something that day that was important. Last night, just after Lucky's death, it came to me what it was! And then I realized there was no time to waste . . .'

'How did Tim Kendal come to kill the wrong woman?'

'Sheer chance. I think his plan was this: Having convinced everybody—and that included Molly herself—that she was mentally unbalanced, and after giving her a sizeable dose of the drug he was using, he told her that

224

between them they were going to clear up all these murder puzzles. But she had got to help him. After everyone was asleep, they would go separately and meet at an agreed spot by the creek.

'He said he had a very good idea who the murderer was, and they would trap him. Molly went off obediently—but she was confused and stupefied with the drug she had been given, and it slowed her up. Tim arrived there first and saw what he thought was Molly. Golden hair and pale green shawl. He came up behind her, put his hand over her mouth, and forced her down into the water and held her there.'

'Nice fellow! But wouldn't it have been easier just to give her an overdose of narcotic?'

'Much easier, of course. But that *might* have given rise to suspicion. All narcotics and sedatives have been very carefully removed from Molly's reach, remember. And if she *had* got hold of a fresh supply, who more likely to have supplied it than her husband? But if, in a fit of despair, she went out and drowned herself whilst her innocent husband slept, the whole thing would be a romantic tragedy, and no one would be likely to suggest that she had been drowned deliberately. Besides,' added Miss Marple, 'murderers always find it difficult to keep things simple. They can't keep themselves from elaborating.'

'You seem convinced you know all there is to be known about murderers! So you believe Tim didn't know he had killed the wrong woman?'

Miss Marple shook her head.

'He didn't even look at her face, just hurried off as

quickly as he could, let an hour elapse, then started to organize a search for her, playing the part of a distracted husband.'

'But what the devil was Lucky doing hanging about the creek in the middle of the night?'

Miss Marple gave an embarrassed little cough.

'It is possible, I think, that she was—er—waiting to meet someone.'

'Edward Hillingdon?'

'Oh *no*,' said Miss Marple. 'That's all over, I wondered whether—just possibly—she might have been waiting for Jackson.'

'Waiting for *Jackson*?'

'I've noticed her—look at him once or twice,' murmured Miss Marple, averting her eyes.

Mr Rafiel whistled.

'My Tom Cat Jackson! I wouldn't put it past him! Tim must have had a shock later when he found he'd killed the wrong woman.'

'Yes, indeed. He must have felt quite desperate. Here was Molly alive and wandering about. And the story he'd circulated so carefully about her mental condition wouldn't stand up for a moment once she got into the hands of competent mental specialists. And once she told her damning story of his having asked her to meet him at the creek, where would Tim Kendal be? He'd only one hope— to finish off Molly as quickly as possible. Then there was a very good chance that everyone would believe that Molly, in a fit of mania, had drowned Lucky, and had then, horrified by what she had done, taken her own life.'

'And it was then,' said Mr Rafiel, 'that you decided to play Nemesis, eh?'

He leaned back suddenly and roared with laughter. 'It's a damned good joke,' he said. 'If you knew what you looked like that night with that fluffy pink wool all round your head, standing there and saying you were Nemesis! I'll never forget it!'

Epilogue

The time had come and Miss Marple was waiting at the airport for her plane. Quite a lot of people had come to see her off. The Hillingdons had left already. Gregory Dyson had flown to one of the other islands and the rumour had come that he was devoting himself to an Argentinian widow. Señora de Caspearo had returned to South America.

Molly had come to see Miss Marple off. She was pale and thin but she had weathered the shock of her discovery bravely and with the help of one of Mr Rafiel's nominees whom he had wired for to England, she was carrying on with the running of the hotel.

'Do you good to be busy,' Mr Rafiel observed. 'Keep you from thinking. Got a good thing here.'

'You don't think the murders—'

'People love murders when they're all cleared up,' Mr Rafiel had assured her. 'You carry on, girl, and keep your heart up. Don't distrust all men because you've met one bad lot.'

'You sound like Miss Marple,' Molly had said, 'she's always telling me Mr Right will come along one day.'

Mr Rafiel grinned at this sentiment. So Molly was there and the two Prescotts and Mr Rafiel, of course, and Esther—an Esther who looked older and sadder and to whom Mr Rafiel was quite often unexpectedly kind. Jackson also was very much to the fore, pretending to be looking after Miss Marple's baggage. He was all smiles these days and let it be known that he had come into money.

There was a hum in the sky. The plane was arriving. Things were somewhat informal here. There was no 'taking your place by Channel 8' or Channel 9. You just walked out from the little flower-covered pavilion on to the tarmac.

'Goodbye, darling Miss Marple.' Molly kissed her.

'Goodbye. Do try and come and visit us.' Miss Prescott shook her warmly by the hand.

'It has been a great pleasure to know you,' said the Canon. 'I second my sister's invitation most warmly.'

'All the best, Madam,' said Jackson, 'and remember any time you want any massage free, just you send me a line and we'll make an appointment.'

Only Esther Walters turned slightly away when the time came for goodbyes. Miss Marple did not force one upon her. Mr Rafiel came last. He took her hand.

'*Ave Caesar, nos morituri te salutamus*,' he said.

'I'm afraid,' said Miss Marple, 'I don't know very much Latin.'

'But you understand that?'

'Yes.' She said no more. She knew quite well what he was telling her.

'It has been a great pleasure to know you,' she said.

Then she walked across the tarmac and got into the plane.